She felt [illegible]*!*

The night w[illegible]re.
The sounds [illegible]
to fade into [illegible] desire
surrounded t[illegible] both. Although the light wind reminded Claire they were outside, the stones and the darkness concealed them. They were alone. And Claire's need for Will, for his touch, his taste, had taken control.

This time, though, she wanted him inside her. "Make love to me," she murmured. "Now. Please, Will. I need you."

Moments later he was filling her completely. She arched against him, driving him even deeper, feeling a delicious sense of power...of rightness. Neither one of them seemed to be able to hold back. Will drove into her, again and again. Claire cried out with pleasure, but the sounds were swallowed by the night and the noise of the crowd.

It was the most passionate sex she'd ever experienced.

And if the rest of her nights were like this, she was never going home....

Blaze™

Dear Reader,

As you can see by the title of this book, I'm back in Ireland again! After writing twelve Mighty Quinn books, I just can't seem to leave the "auld sod" behind. And this from a girl who has only a few drops of Irish blood in her (from my fifth great-grandfather, Patrick Doolin).

Doing Ireland! was a chance to indulge in a bit of Irish magic. While visiting Ireland a few years back, I found the land and the people entirely captivating, so it wasn't difficult to imagine my hero, Will Donovan, as a sexy innkeeper living on an island off the coast of County Kerry. When a midwestern girl arrives on the island, Will gets a chance to live out a fantasy. And that's what a vacation love affair ought to be—pure fantasy.

I hope you enjoy this holiday in Ireland. And who knows? Maybe I'll be going back soon to find a few more Quinn cousins.

Happy reading,

Kate Hoffmann

KATE HOFFMANN

Doing Ireland!

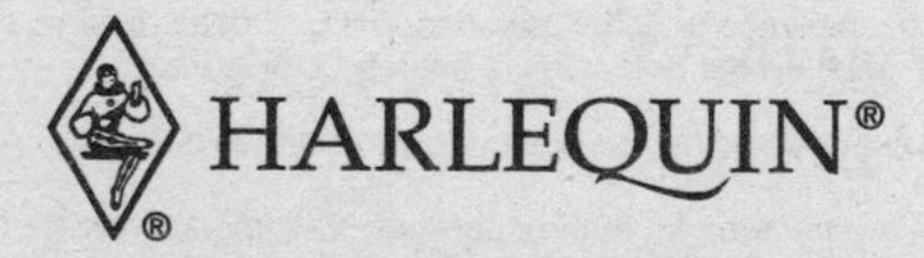

TORONTO • NEW YORK • LONDON
AMSTERDAM • PARIS • SYDNEY • HAMBURG
STOCKHOLM • ATHENS • TOKYO • MILAN • MADRID
PRAGUE • WARSAW • BUDAPEST • AUCKLAND

ISBN-13: 978-0-373-79344-0
ISBN-10: 0-373-79344-8

DOING IRELAND!

This edition published by arrangement with Harlequin Books S.A.

www.eHarlequin.com

Printed in U.S.A.

ABOUT THE AUTHOR

Kate Hoffmann's first book was published by Harlequin Books in 1993. Since then she's written over fifty more titles, including the popular MIGHTY QUINN series. Her books, known for their mix of humor and sensuality, have appeared in the Harlequin Temptation and Blaze lines. Kate lives in a small town in Wisconsin, with her cats and her computer. Besides writing, she works with high-school students in theater and musical activities. She also enjoys golf, movies, music of all kinds and genealogy research.

Books by Kate Hoffmann

HARLEQUIN BLAZE

234—SINFULLY SWEET
"Simply Scrumptious"
279—THE MIGHTY QUINNS: MARCUS
285—THE MIGHTY QUINNS: IAN
291—THE MIGHTY QUINNS: DECLAN

HARLEQUIN SINGLE TITLES (The Quinns)

REUNITED
THE PROMISE
THE LEGACY

HARLEQUIN TEMPTATION

847—THE MIGHTY QUINNS: CONOR
851—THE MIGHTY QUINNS: DYLAN
855—THE MIGHTY QUINNS: BRENDAN
933—THE MIGHTY QUINNS: LIAM
937—THE MIGHTY QUINNS: BRIAN
941—THE MIGHTY QUINNS: SEAN
963—LEGALLY MINE
988—HOT & BOTHERED
1017—WARM & WILLING

1

THE BOAT SKIMMED over the choppy gray water, sending a gentle spray into the air to land on Claire O'Connor's face. She brushed a damp strand of hair from her eyes, then fixed her gaze on the small island in the distance, a hazy bump on the horizon.

The Isle of Trall. She'd left Chicago twenty-four hours earlier and now that she was nearing her destination, Claire realized she'd come on a fool's errand. "I must be crazy," she murmured.

"What's that, lass?"

Claire glanced over at Billy Boyle, the captain of the mail boat, and forced a smile. "Nothing," she murmured.

"If ye step inside, you won't be gettin' so damp."

"That's all right," Claire said. Perhaps the cold and damp were exactly what she needed to shake a little sense into herself. So much had happened in the past two days she'd hardly had a chance to think clearly. She'd lost her boyfriend, her job and her apartment all in one six-hour period. As a result, she'd begun a quest to get them all back in one crazy act of desperation, an act that brought her to a tiny island off the western coast of Ireland.

"We don't see too many single passengers makin' the trip to Trall," Captain Billy said. "Mostly couples. It's a romantic destination, ye know. Not really a place for people to visit on their own."

Her grandmother, Orla O'Connor, had told her of the island, and of the legend, but Claire wanted to hear it again, from someone who had more than just fifty-year-old evidence of its existence. "Why is that?" she asked.

"They come hoping to find the Druid spring. It's in all the tour books. It's said that if a couple drinks the water, they will be bound together for life. Eternal love and all that. You ask me, I think it's bollocks."

"Do you know where this spring is?" she asked.

Captain Billy shook his head. "I'm the one who should have been lookin'. I've had meself three wives and not one of them is still warmin' me bed."

Claire turned her attention back to the island. She'd been under the assumption that the location of the spring would be posted on every roadside in Trall, with huge signs and arrows pointing the way, and maybe even a modern visitors center. Her grandmother had said nothing about having to search for it! "Is there anyone who knows where it is?"

Captain Billy considered her question for a long moment, then shrugged. "I'd suppose Sorcha Mulroony would know. She's a Druid princess or… priestess, I think she calls herself. Me, I think she's a bit barmy. But she fancies herself the keeper of all the island's magic. You could ask her, but she charges a steep price for her services."

"Her services?"

"Soothsaying, curses, spells, she does it all. I bought a curse from her last year. Cost me fifty euros, it did. There was a tosser from Dingle who was tryin' to get the contract for the mail boat by cuttin' my price. Sorcha cursed his boat and it sank in the harbor the very next day."

"Did you ever think maybe she just poked a hole in the side of his boat and that's why it sank?"

Billy thought about the possibility as if it had never occurred to him before. Then he shrugged. "I don't care what she did. That bloke isn't haulin' mail to Trall, is he now?"

"I suppose he isn't," she said with a smile. Claire wrapped her corduroy jacket more tightly around her, watching as the island grew larger and larger on the horizon. "Can you recommend a place to stay on Trall?"

"There's a lovely inn to the north of town. The Ivybrook out on Cove Road. This time of year, there should be rooms available. Will Donovan runs it. His family has been on the island for generations. He's a celebrity of sorts, he is."

"Famous? For what?"

"Oh, we don't gossip about our neighbors on Trall." Billy frowned. "But maybe this isn't gossip, more in the line of news. A few years back, he was named one of Ireland's most eligible bachelors. Got his picture in a fancy magazine for it."

"Interesting," Claire said.

"His great-grandfather was the first to run the inn. T'was an old manor house at one time. A summer home for some posh Brit. Will left the island for university and we thought we'd seen the last of 'im. Then three years ago, he comes back to Trall to run the inn. His folks, Mick and Maeve Donovan, wanted to be closer to their daughter and their grandkids, so they were off to Dublin. Island life seems to suit Will. That's not gossip, it's fact."

"I probably should have called ahead for a reservation."

"I haven't brought any tourists out to the island in the past three days," the captain said. "So I don't think ye'll have a problem. There'll be more folks coming in for the Samhain celebration later this week."

"Oh, I'll be gone by then," Claire said. "I'm just staying a night, maybe two."

"If ye don't find Will at the inn, there's a key under the flowerpot next to the door. Just let yourself in."

"Why would he lock the door if everyone knows where the key is?"

"'Cause of Dickie O'Malley. He's got a farm south of town and he's got no hot runnin' water. So he wanders into town looking for a place to take a bath. Dickie is a dirty bugger and he always leaves a mess. Uses every clean towel in the place. He also drinks every last drop of whiskey before he leaves. I guess you could say it's his callin' card. That's not gossip, lass, it's just fact."

They passed the rest of the trip in silence, Claire sitting at the stern of the boat, trying to make out details of the island as they approached. Suddenly, her reasons for coming to Trall seemed so silly. She'd come to find a magic spring that would make her boyfriend love her again.

The sequence of events leading to this moment had been burned indelibly into her brain. She'd risen just yesterday morning, thinking it was a day like any other. Eric had left for the office early and rather than ride in with him, Claire had decided to sleep a little longer and take the train. It was only moments after she got up that she found the note, a fluorescent green sticky stuck to the bathroom mirror. *It's over. I'm sorry. Goodbye.*

Eric had been pensive and moody for the past month, but Claire had assumed he was leading up to a proposal of marriage, not a breakup, especially after she'd found the credit card receipt for a $9,000 purchase at one of Chicago's finest jewelers.

She'd dressed for work, determined to speak to him the moment she arrived at the office. They'd worked at the same advertising agency for four years and had been together for two and a half. He couldn't be serious about breaking up, she'd told herself.

But when she'd arrived at work, she'd found the agency in complete chaos. A company meeting had been called early that morning to inform the staff that the agency had just been bought out by a larger firm. Half the employees would be without jobs. She was promptly called into the creative director's office and told she was officially unemployed. It was only then she'd learned Eric had tendered his resignation the day before and was already gone, his office empty of his personal effects, his whereabouts unknown.

As if things couldn't get worse, when she returned home a few hours later, she found an overnight envelope propped up against her apartment door. Inside was a notice that her building was being converted to condos and she was welcome to buy at a price an unemployed advertising art director could never afford.

Claire had always been so careful in planning her life, from finding the right man to getting a job at the best agency in town to living in a beautiful apartment in a trendy Chicago neighborhood. She watched her diet, choosing organic foods from the grocery store, and she worked out religiously, four times a week at her health club. She even did volunteer work once a week with an after-school program. How could her life possibly have gone so bad in such a short time?

"When it rains, it pours," her grandmother had told her as Claire had sat numbly on her sofa. And then, Orla O'Connor had given her granddaughter a simple solution. Win back the man in your life first. The rest will fall into place. When Claire had asked how, Orla had a ready answer. A trip to Ireland, to the Isle of Trall, would solve all her problems.

"And here I am," she murmured. On a boat to Trall.

Captain Billy steered into a calm harbor and deftly maneuvered the boat up to an empty dock. When it bumped against the wood pilings, he jumped off and secured the lines, then helped Claire onto the dock. A moment later, her luggage was sitting at her feet.

"The mail boat leaves at noon, Monday to Friday. You can catch a ride back with me or take the car ferry. That makes three trips a day, every day."

"Which way is the inn?" Claire asked.

"'Bout a mile down the road," Billy said, pointing off

to the north. He glanced up at the sky. "You'd better hurry along. It looks like we're due for a spot of rain."

"Isn't there a taxi?"

This time he glanced at his watch. "Well, there usually is, if guests are expected, but you weren't expected, now, were you? Dougal Fraser runs the island's taxi service, but it's nearly 4:00 p.m. I suspect he's already well into his second pint at the pub. That's it just over there. The Jolly Farmer, it's called."

"Could you give me a ride to the inn?"

The captain shook his head. "Oh, no. That would be puttin' a toe onto Dougal's turf and he wouldn't take kindly to me doin' that. We have our own little rules here on the island and stealin' a man's livin' is one that we never break. Besides, I keep my car on the mainland. No need for it here. There's nowhere to go on this island."

"And if he's not there? Am I expected to walk a mile with my suitcases?"

"Oh, I'm sure someone will come along and offer you a ride, then. Just wave them down and tell them where you're going."

Claire watched as Billy grabbed a sack from the boat and hefted it over his shoulder. "Come along, I'll show you the way." They walked to the end of the dock and Billy pointed to a small white-washed building on the corner of the cobblestone street. "Walk right in there and ask for Dougal. Hurry along now, before ye get wet."

The light rain had turned to a steady downpour as Claire reached the door of the pub. She wiped the water from her eyes and walked inside. It took a moment for her eyes to adjust to the dimly lit interior, but when they did, she saw the bartender and two patrons staring at her with curious gazes.

"I'm looking for Dougal Fraser?" Claire said.

WILL DONOVAN tossed another sod of peat onto the hearth in the spacious parlor of the inn, then stared into the flames. The peat flamed, sending a welcome rush of warmth into the chilly room.

"Fetch me another whiskey," Sorcha murmured, staring at him through a tumble of coppery-red hair.

He glanced over his shoulder to see her holding out the crystal tumbler, snuggled into her usual spot on the sofa. Her lips curved into a smile he knew all too well, one she'd used on any number of men to great success, weaving her spell about them until they were defenseless against her charms. Will had fallen prey the summer he'd returned to the island three years ago, indulging in a brief but passionate affair with Sorcha.

But in the end, after six tempestuous months, they realized they'd made much better friends than lovers. Until just last year, Sorcha had still been convinced he was the only man for her. So she had used every Druid power she possessed to make his life miserable. In fact, he still carried one or two of her curses. "Why should I fetch you a whiskey?" he asked, relaxing into an overstuffed chair across from the sofa.

"You're the host here. I'm the guest."

"And you invited yourself to supper," Will reminded her.

"Please, fetch me a whiskey," Sorcha whined. "Or I'll put a feckin' curse on you, Will Donovan."

Will crossed the room and grabbed her glass, then strolled over to the small table that held the decanter. He poured a small measure into the tumbler and returned to the sofa. But when Sorcha held out her hand, he pulled the whiskey back. "I'll give you this drink if you do me a small kindness in return."

Sorcha sat up on her heels, brushing her hair out of her pale eyes. "This sounds interesting. What's wrong? Has it been a while since you've had some?"

He wagged his finger at her. "We're not going to go there, Sorcha," he muttered. "We've been there before and it didn't work."

"I know. But this time we can just have a shag. We won't bother with the relationship."

"Let's be honest. You devour men. You require that they worship you and wait on you and satisfy you until they're nothing but blithering fools. And then you toss them aside for someone new."

Sorcha's lips pressed into a pout. "How can you say that? I love men."

"Maybe a little too much," Will said.

"If you're going to insult me, then give me my whiskey. I feel like getting pissed."

"Not until you do something for me."

"What do you want? Obviously not my body. I should be humiliated, but I'm not. I've come to think of you as a...dare I say it? A brother?" She giggled. "A very hot brother. Oh, hell, I'd probably be riddled with guilt if we slept together again. I do have some standards to maintain."

"I want you to lift the curse you put on me," he said.

A satisfied grin curled her lips. "I didn't think you believed in my powers."

"I don't."

"Which curse?" she asked.

Will groaned. "How many are there?"

There was a long moment before Sorcha answered. "Two. No, three." She paused. "No, wait, I lifted that one after you helped me fix my car. Two," she said.

"And what were they?"

"Well…one was so you'd never meet another woman as beautiful and sexy as I am. And the other had to do with your…performance in the bedroom." She slowly raised her index finger, then let it curl up again. "A willy-wilting curse for Will."

He frowned. Since they'd ended their relationship, his luck with women hadn't been great, but he'd still been able to perform when called upon. He'd had three serious relationships in the past two years and all had ended after only a few months. In between, he'd indulged in an occasional one- or two-night stand with old girlfriends in London or Dublin. Living on an island offered few possibilities for regular or casual sex. That could only be found on the mainland.

"In the spirit of our newfound friendship," Will said, "I want you to reverse both curses. Right now. In front of me."

Sorcha sighed and grabbed the whiskey from his hand. "All right." She swallowed her drink in one gulp, then sat up straight and closed her eyes, tipping forward until her red hair fell like a curtain around her face. Slowly, she began to rock back and forth, mumbling a string of words that Will recognized as Gaelic. Though he knew a fair bit of the language, he didn't understand what she was saying. Suddenly, she opened her eyes. "I'm starved," she said. "I need taytos. I have to have nourishment for this to work." Then she closed her eyes and began to mutter again.

Will wandered back to the kitchen and grabbed a bag of potato crisps. When he returned to the parlor, Sorcha was lying down on the sofa. He handed her the bag of crisps and she tore it open, then popped one into her mouth. "God, I'm hungry," she muttered. "Do you have any chocolate?"

"We're going to eat in an hour. Are you done?"

She stuffed two more crisps into her mouth, then nodded. "Yes. You are now completely curse-free." She paused. "Well, not entirely. I did a wee counterspell, just something between two good friends."

"Sorcha, you promised."

"This is a good spell. The next woman you meet will madly desire you and you'll have a wildly passionate sexual encounter within twenty-four hours. She will stop at nothing to get into your trousers and have a go."

A frantic knocking sounded through the quiet of the parlor and Sorcha giggled. "Ah! The spell has worked. It's herself! I wonder who it could be? The single women on this island are a sad lot, except, of course, for me. I suppose Eveleen Dooly wouldn't be so bad in bed. And then there's Mary Carlisle. She's old but she's sprightly."

"At least Eveleen wouldn't curse me," Will muttered. "While I answer the door, you remove the spell. Am I clear?"

"Quite," Sorcha said. "Just walk slowly. It'll take some time. It was a very complex spell."

Will strolled out to the front hall, then waited a bit before he opened the front door. Standing on the steps was a woman, drenched by the rain, her shoes covered in mud.

"It's about time," she muttered, pale hair plastered to her face. "I'm soaked to the skin. And I couldn't find the key. It's supposed to be under the flowerpot."

"I'm sorry," Will said, reaching out to grab her bags. "Sorcha must have used…well, never mind. Come in, please. Welcome to the Ivybrook Inn."

She walked inside, tracking mud across the parquet floor of the hall. Glancing back, she noticed what she'd done, then cursed softly, struggling out of her ruined shoes. "I couldn't find the taxi. He was supposed to be at the pub and he wasn't. Some farmer offered to give me a ride on his horse. Good thing, because an Irish mile seems to be a lot longer than an American mile. It took me forever to get here." She picked up her shoes, her wet clothes making a puddle around her. "I need a room."

Will studied her as he stepped behind the front desk. It was hard to tell what she looked like. She'd tied a scarf around her head to ward off the rain and her hair hung in a stringy mess over her eyes. One cheek was muddy and the other was stained with mascara.

Her jacket and jeans were so baggy and waterlogged that her shape was indistinct beneath them. She did have very pretty feet, Will mused, and her toenails were painted a bright pink. And she looked young, probably not much older than twenty-five or twenty-six. Will watched as she rummaged through her purse.

"You're American?" he asked.

She shoved her hair back and met his gaze for the first time. Tiny droplets clung to her lashes and she blinked several times, sending rivulets down rosy cheeks. "I—I'm sorry, what did you ask?"

"American?" Will repeated softly, his gaze falling to her lips.

"Yes. Is that a problem?"

When he looked up, he found himself staring into sparkling turquoise eyes. She held out a credit card. "No, not at all," he said, taking the card. "I was just curious. You sounded…American."

A tiny smile twitched at the corners of her mouth. "That's probably because I am." A shudder ran through her and she rubbed her arms. "So, may I have a room? I'd really like to get out of these clothes and—"

"Yes, of course," Will said. "And I'd like to get you out of those…I mean, I'm sure you'd be more comfortable if you took your clothes off…and put others back on." He grabbed the key for the nicest room on the second floor. "Room seven," he said. Will reached out and grabbed her hand, then put the key in her palm. Her skin was damp and cool to the touch and he let his fingers linger, his thumb slowly caressing the inside of her wrist. "Top of the stairs and to your left. It's at the end of the hall. All our rooms are en suite."

"What does that mean?" she muttered, staring down at the key.

He grabbed her shoes from her hand. "They all have

their own bathrooms. Seven has a very large tub with a shower. Why don't you go on up and I'll bring your luggage and shoes after I've had a chance to dry them off."

"All right," she said. She gently pulled her hand from his grip, then started toward the stairs.

"What is your name?" Will called.

She spun around. "What?"

"Your name. For the register."

"It's on the card," she replied. "O'Connor. Claire O'Connor from Chicago. Illinois."

"Welcome to the Ivybrook Inn, Miss O'Connor," he said, glancing down at the credit card. "I'm Will Donovan."

She nodded, then trudged up the stairs, her clothes dripping as she climbed. When he turned to tend to her bags, he found Sorcha leaning up against the doorjamb to the front parlor, clutching the bag of crisps to her chest and munching thoughtfully. "An American. Pretty thing, that," she murmured, nodding toward the stairs. "I hear American girls are positively wild in the sack."

"I don't seduce the guests," he said. "Don't you have some potions to brew? Go home, Sorcha."

"Too bad about the curse," she murmured. "I'm afraid you were a bit too fast answering the door. I didn't have a chance to remove the spell." She grinned as she popped another crisp into her mouth. "She's definitely worth a shag or two, Will. I think I'll just be going now." She walked over to Will, straightened his collar and smoothed his hair. "Just remember to be nice and to use a Johnny. Good sex is safe sex."

"Get out," Will muttered.

She grabbed her mackintosh from the coat tree in the hall and slipped into it. "Have fun, Wills. You can thank me later," she said.

Will walked back to the kitchen to fetch some rags, then cleaned up the mess Claire O'Connor had made in the entry hall. Her shoes were ruined, but he dried off her suitcases and carried them upstairs.

Her door was slightly ajar and he knocked softly. "Miss O'Connor?"

There was no answer. Will peeked inside and found the room empty. He placed the suitcases next to the bed, and turned back to the door. As he did, he glanced into the bathroom and his breath caught in his throat. The door was open just far enough for him to see her lying in the tub.

He froze, unwilling to invade her privacy. But then Will realized she was sound asleep, her arms draped over the sides, her head resting on the edge of the old clawfoot tub as water still poured out of the faucet.

Her pale hair was brushed away from her face and he found himself transfixed by the simple beauty of her profile, her upturned nose, her lush lips. He noticed a tiny sprinkling of freckles across her cheeks. His gaze drifted down, to the soft flesh of her breasts, rosy from the rising water in the tub.

Desire warmed his blood and he fought the impulse to step closer. Innkeepers had certain standards they kept to and spying on a female guest while she was in her bath went way beyond acceptable behavior. But then, what if Sorcha was right? What if this woman was meant to be his anyway?

She stirred slightly, then sighed, her lips parting as she sank a bit deeper into the bath. Will backed up and grabbed the suitcases, setting them closer to the door. When he reached the hallway, he drew a deep breath and leaned back against the wall. If the tub overflowed, he'd have a reason to return, but for now, he'd keep to the hall.

The image of her naked body whirled in his head and he felt himself growing hard at the thought of touching her. Will groaned in frustration. Sure, it had been a while. And there had been the occasional fantasy about a sexy female guest, a beautiful woman with no inhibitions intent on seducing him, the inn quiet and empty, as it was now. But he had never once considered making the fantasy real.

Perhaps she'd only stay for one night. Or perhaps her boyfriend or fiancé or husband would be joining her tomorrow. Besides, he didn't believe Sorcha Mulroony had even an ounce of mystical power. He'd be polite and accommodating and hospitable to Claire O'Connor. Nothing more.

THE BATH WAS LUKEWARM by the time Claire crawled out. She wrapped herself in a thick cotton towel, then walked into the bedroom. Her suitcases had been placed next to the door, and for a moment, she wondered how the innkeeper had slipped into her room without her noticing.

An image of the man flashed in her mind and Claire recalled her reaction when she first looked into his eyes. There were obviously handsome men scattered all over the world, but somehow, the fates had blessed the Isle of Trall with a truly beautiful specimen. But why was one of Ireland's most eligible bachelors living here?

She smiled as she sat down on the edge of the bed, wrapping the towel more tightly around her. Back at her job, she'd stared at thousands of images—male models, everyday guys, celebrities—trying to figure out what it was that made one man merely attractive and another devastatingly sexy.

Will Donovan belonged in the latter category. He possessed features that were in perfect balance. He wasn't pretty, he was gorgeous. And it wasn't the straight nose or the expressive mouth or the eyes that were an odd mix of green and gold. It was the way he wore his looks, so casually, as if he weren't aware of the effect they had on women.

He hadn't shaved in two or three days and it looked as if he preferred his fingers to a comb when it came to fixing his hair. Everything about him was comfortably rumpled, as if he'd just rolled out of bed, even the lazy way he looked at her with half-hooded eyes.

Claire retrieved a bottle of scented lotion from her suitcase and rested her foot on the edge of the bed as she rubbed some of the product over her legs. With any other man, she might not have given him a second thought. After all, it had been just one day since her relationship with Eric had ended. And she'd come to Ireland to save that relationship.

She was in a foreign country, so of course she'd find a guy like Will Donovan...interesting. Maybe even a bit exotic. That accent, the sound of her name on his lips, the way his gaze drifted between her mouth and her eyes. Lusting after another man now would be a waste of precious time. As long as she was here in Ireland, she'd do what she came to do—save her relationship with Eric. After all, she and Eric were meant for each other.

Claire had known from the moment she'd met him. All her life, she had waited for the perfect man. She'd even made a list of all the attributes she sought in a husband and Eric had fulfilled every last one of them.

Careful planning and detailed lists had been Claire's specialty since she was a young girl. A shrink would probably tell her that it was simply a way of coping with a chaotic childhood. She'd grown up in a tiny three-bedroom house, with five older brothers, and parents who did little to control the boys. It was noisy and messy and she was almost always ignored when competing against their boisterous antics.

So Claire often escaped to her grandmother's house, where it was quiet and pretty, and she could talk about important matters, like all the things she was going to do with her life. Her grandmother had encouraged her to write it all down in a little journal. "Only when you write it down will it become true," she had said. Later, as each of her dreams were fulfilled, Claire would tick them off in the journal.

Claire tossed the lotion on the bed and grabbed her bags. As she unpacked, she neatly arranged her clothes in the antique dresser against the far wall. She found her birth control pills in a side pocket and popped one out of the package and into her mouth.

She and Eric would be together again. She had to believe that.

As she passed the leaded glass windows that lined one wall, a draft chilled her, goose bumps prickling her arms. She found a match on the mantel and lit the crumpled paper beneath the oddly shaped logs. Warmth from the fire began to seep into her skin and a sharp scent hung in the air. But at the same time, the room started to fill with smoke. Claire realized she hadn't opened the flue and scrambled to find a knob or a lever.

It wasn't on the outside of the fireplace and she couldn't see it on the inside through the smoke. She ran to the window and threw it open, then tore off her towel and began to fan the smoke out the window.

The smoke continued to pour out of the fireplace and Claire realized she'd have to smother the fire to make it stop. She beat at the flames with the damp towel and the fire was nearly out when the smoke alarm went off.

Frantically, she searched the room for the alarm, hoping to disable it before Will Donovan responded. But a moment later, he burst into the smoky room, a fire extinguisher in his hand. Claire screamed and held the scorched towel up to her naked body.

"What the hell is going on?" In three easy strides, he reached the fireplace and smothered the remainder of the fire with foam from the extinguisher. He turned to her, a look of concern etched on his face. "Are you all right?"

"Yes," Claire said. "I just—why would someone lay out a fire and not open the flue?"

He stared at her, his gaze raking over her body. Claire

clutched the towel more tightly to her chest, fumbling as she wrapped one end around her hip.

"Why would someone put match to peat without checking the flue first?" he asked.

"It's—it's freezing in here," she countered.

"The window is open." He walked across the room and closed it, Claire scampering to stand against the wall. Will grabbed the bedspread from the bed and held it out in front of him. Hesitantly, Claire stepped forward and he wrapped it around her body, enveloping her in a soft cocoon.

"I suppose I'm going to have to give you another room," he murmured as he gently rubbed her arms. "You can't sleep in here."

"I'm sorry," she said, risking a glance up at him. Tears of frustration pushed at the corners of her eyes. She was tired, she was cold, her life had become a huge mess and all she really wanted to do was crawl into bed and cry for the next day or two. He had no idea what it was taking to hold herself together.

He looked down and their gazes met—and locked. Claire opened her mouth to speak, to apologize for her emotional state, but then couldn't remember what she'd intended to say. She heard him draw in a sharp breath as his gaze fell to her lips. She knew what was about to happen and simply waited, unwilling to stop him.

"You're sure you're all right," he whispered, leaning closer.

"Fine," she replied in a strangled voice.

Claire's heart slammed in her chest and she closed her eyes and tried to maintain her composure. But Will took her action as his cue and a moment later, his mouth covered hers. It wasn't the typical first kiss, clumsy and a bit tentative. Instead, he kissed her as if he'd been doing it for years, possessing her mouth as if it had always belonged to him, his tongue teasing at hers, challenging her to respond.

The kiss seemed to go on forever, growing deeper and more passionate as it continued. She couldn't remember ever being kissed like this, with such reckless abandon and unfettered intensity. Claire felt his hands slide from her shoulders to her hips, the quilt slipping down between their bodies.

A tiny moan slipped from her throat as she pressed her hips into his, fumbling to maintain some semblance of modesty. His hands came back to her face, cupping her cheeks in his palms. She didn't want it to end, the pleasure surging up inside of her, the crazy sensations coursing through her body. But at the same time, Claire knew that kissing a near stranger while wearing just a bedspread was probably a mistake.

When he finally drew away, she gulped down a deep breath and opened her eyes. She found Will staring at her, a perplexed expression wrinkling his brow. "Jaysus," he murmured. He stepped back and raked his hand through his hair. "What the hell."

Claire swallowed hard, clutching the bedspread to her body. "Wh-why did you do that?"

"I don't know," he replied. "I just—" Will cursed softly. "I don't know. Did you not want me to do that? Because, I got the feeling you did. Was I wrong?"

"No," Claire replied. "I mean, yes. I was just surprised, that's all. It was...unexpected."

"But welcomed? Please, tell me it was welcomed."

Claire thought about her answer for a moment. Should she tell the truth? "Yes," she finally said. "At the least it wasn't unwelcome."

"Good." A smile twitched at his lips. "I guess I'll leave you to get dressed." Will glanced around the room. "You're not going to start any more fires are you, Miss O'Connor?"

She shook her head. "Not right now. And you don't have to call me Miss O'Connor. I mean, considering you just...well, you know. Call me Claire."

"All right. Claire?"

"Yes, Claire," she said.

"Save the fires for later, Claire," he said, nodding. "If you're hungry, I have supper downstairs. And after that, I'll find you another room. A warmer room." He wrinkled his nose. "And one that doesn't smell of smoke."

"Thank you," Claire said.

He stepped back, but not before reaching up and brushing a strand of hair from her eyes. When the door closed behind him, she sank down on the edge of the bed. Smoke still clouded the room and for a heartbeat, she wondered if she'd imagined what had happened between them, if it had all been part of some bizarre, jet-lag-induced fantasy.

She touched her lips and found them damp. This was a disturbing turn of events. How was she supposed to react? She didn't feel indignant or insulted. Nor did she feel guilty or ashamed. In truth, there was a nice, warm sensation deep inside of her, something she hadn't felt in a very long time.

There was definitely an attraction between them. What woman wouldn't be attracted? Will Donovan was undeniably handsome. And very different from… well, from Eric.

Her relationship with Eric hadn't been entirely perfect. In truth, lately it had become ordinary, not that she'd realized it until this very moment. It had been months since he'd made her heart skip a beat or her breath come in tiny gasps, months since he'd kissed her with that type of passion. And now this stranger, this Irishman, had accomplished both in a matter of minutes.

And there were things about Eric that had begun to bug her—his vanity, for one. His selfishness. She couldn't remember the last time they'd made love where she'd been completely and utterly satisfied. Will Donovan was probably the kind of man who'd leave a woman pleasantly, thoroughly exhausted.

Claire jumped up from the bed and rummaged through her suitcases, searching for something nice to wear. She hadn't planned on experiencing this particular element on her trip, so she'd brought along comfortable clothes—jeans, T-shirts and sweaters. She decided on a pair of black pencil-leg jeans and a translucent white silk blouse. To add a hint of interest, she'd wear a black bra beneath. She retrieved her hair dryer and the converter plug she'd brought along, then headed to the bathroom to get ready.

A half hour later, her hair was dry and her lipstick

was on. Claire gave herself one last critical look in the mirror, then sighed as she stared at her reflection. What was she expecting? This was crazy! Did she plan to seduce this man over dinner? Grabbing a tissue, she wiped off her lipstick and tied her pale hair back with a silk scarf. "You're in love with Eric," she reminded herself. "And he still loves you. He just doesn't realize it."

The inn was quiet as she walked down the stairs. A fire crackled in the front parlor hearth and she walked through the spacious rooms, searching for the dining room. But when she found it, it was dark and empty.

"I thought we could eat in the kitchen. It's nice and warm in there."

Claire glanced up to see a shadowy form standing in the doorway, broad-shouldered, a hip braced against the doorjamb. Her heart fluttered and she cursed inwardly at the unbidden response. All right, there was definitely a spark. But that didn't mean she had to fan it into a raging inferno. She smoothed her hands over her blouse and forced a smile. "Of course. And thank you."

"For what?" he asked.

"For making me dinner."

"You haven't tasted my cooking," he replied with a low chuckle. He held open the door to the butler's pantry and Claire walked through the cabinet-lined room to the kitchen.

Unlike the rest of the house, the kitchen was sleek and modern, with granite countertops and stainless-steel appliances. But an old stone hearth burned brightly with a peat fire, the scent familiar to her now. She walked over to it and held her hands out. "Why am I so cold? The winters in Chicago are brutal, but I don't feel the cold like I do here."

"We live on the ocean. It's damp," Will explained. "That's why it feels colder. There's no getting away from it." Will pulled a stool out from beneath the huge worktable that dominated the center of the kitchen. He nodded his head. "Have a seat."

Claire perched on the stool and watched Will as he moved around the room. She was glad to see that he wasn't going to too much trouble, choosing to make sandwiches. "Do you always cook for your guests?" she asked.

Will shook his head. "Never. When we have guests, our cook and housekeeper, Katie Kelly, comes in and does breakfast. Beyond that we don't serve meals."

She cupped her chin in her hand. "So why are you doing it now?"

He glanced up at her, sending her a devastatingly charming smile. "After what you've been through today, I figured you'd need it. And your only other alternative is the Jolly Farmer and that's noisy and smoky and filled with blokes who haven't seen a woman as flah as you in a very long time."

"Flah?"

"Beautiful," he said.

Claire felt a blush warm her cheeks. It was such an offhand compliment that she wasn't sure how to take it. Did he really think she was beautiful or was he simply humoring a guest?

"So, what brings you to Trall?" he asked.

She hesitated before she answered, unwilling to tell him the truth about her quest. Perhaps, if he'd been a woman, she'd unload her entire sad story. But he wasn't a woman. He was an incredibly attractive man. "Family history," Claire quickly replied. "My grandmother, Orla O'Connor, visited the island a long time ago. She told me about it and so I thought I'd see it for myself."

"There's not much to see," Will said. "There are some shops in the village and there's a stone circle on the west side of the island. Most people come here for the Druid spring, though."

"My grandmother told me about that." She glanced up to find him staring at her. He held her gaze for a long moment, then turned back to his meal preparations.

"Beyond the stone circle, it's Trall's only claim to fame."

"I thought you were famous," Claire said. She let her eyes drift down, from his broad shoulders to his narrow waist, and then lower. Though his jeans were slightly baggy, she could see he had a nice butt. "At least, that's what Captain Billy told me."

"No," Will said, glancing over his shoulder. "That's just a load of rubbish. As for the spring, it's a silly legend that brings tourists to the island, so no one disputes it."

"But everyone knows about it."

"I suppose," Will said. "Everyone benefits from perpetuating the legend, I guess. There aren't that many of us left on the island so we welcome the visitors. Just over five hundred now. We're kind of like one big family. Sometimes a wee bit dysfunctional, but a family nonetheless." He set a plate with a ham sandwich in front of her and followed it with a mug of steaming soup, then went to the refrigerator and grabbed a couple of beers. "You drink Guinness? I have wine, too. Or bottled water?"

"Beer is fine," Claire said.

He opened a bottle and set it down in front of her, then opened his and took a long drink. He had beautiful hands. Claire had always found that she could tell a lot about a man by his hands. His fingers were long and tapered, the kind of hands that might touch a woman with expert effect, dancing over her body until she cried out in—

"You said you were from Chicago?"

Claire swallowed hard. "Y-yes," she said.

"The Windy City?"

"Ummm. Have you ever been to Chicago?"

"I have," Will said. "I remember the lake. A big lake. So big you couldn't see the other side even from the top of that tall building."

"The Sears Tower. That's Lake Michigan," Claire said, munching on the ham sandwich. "What were you doing in Chicago?"

"Business," he murmured. Will studied the label on his beer bottle, scratching at it with his thumbnail. Claire found herself watching his hands again, her pulse quickening. "A very exciting place, that."

She cleared her throat, determined to steer the conversation in a different direction. "Tell me more about the spring," she said.

"The water is said to be blessed by the Druids, although there's only one Druid on the island and I have cause to doubt her credentials. They say if two people drink from the same cup, they'll share eternal love."

"Really?"

He nodded. "Couples usually come here before they go see a marriage counselor, hoping to find answers to their problems. And honeymooners like to come, too."

"And do you know where this spring is?" Claire asked.

"There are springs all over the island." He gave her a sly look. "It doesn't exist. It's just a legend. We Irish love our legends."

She took a sip of her beer. "But if it doesn't exist, then why do people keep coming?"

"If you had a chance at eternal love, wouldn't you go after it?" He laughed softly. "That was a rhetorical question."

"So no one really knows where it is?"

"Oh, I'm sure some might think they've found it. But I've never seen proof that any of the water on this island does more than quench a man's thirst."

He smiled and Claire felt her stomach flutter. This island was already working its magic upon her. She felt alive and uninhibited, as if anything were possible. She wanted to jump out of her chair and kiss Will Donovan again. Her fingers ached to touch his rumpled hair and her body craved his warmth. There was just too much about him that she found attractive.

"How's the sandwich?" he asked.

"It's very good," she said. "Everything here is… good." And Claire had a very distinct feeling that it would get even better before the night was over.

2

SHE WAS BEAUTIFUL. Perhaps the most beautiful woman he'd ever met. Will watched her as she took a sip of her wine, then snuggled back into the pillows on the opposite end of the sofa.

After dinner, they'd moved to the front parlor where Will had opened a bottle of cabernet and stoked the fire in the hearth. Though business had slowed down once the warmer days of summer had ended, for once, Will was grateful not to have other guests to tend to. Right now, he wanted to focus all of his attention on Claire.

She was different than any woman he'd ever met. Since all the publicity that followed his appointment as one of Ireland's most eligible, it had been difficult to meet women who were really interested in him and not his money. In fact, all the energy spent trying to discern a woman's true motives had made dating a chore.

He had managed one serious relationship, with a beautiful woman whom he thought he might marry. But the moment she found out Will was planning to sell his business and move back to Trall, she tossed him over for a hard-partying football player.

To Claire, he was just a guy who ran an inn—and he liked that. "How long do you plan to stay?" he asked.

She took another sip of her wine and sighed sleepily. "A day or two. I want to see something of the island."

"You'll be comfortable here."

She met his gaze. "Yes, I think I will." Covering her mouth, Claire stifled a yawn then sent him an apologetic smile. "I'm sorry. I can't seem to keep my eyes open. I have no idea what time it is back home, but I know I've been awake for too long. I should get some sleep."

Will wasn't anxious for their evening to end, but he was curious to see *how* it would end. Would they indulge in another kiss? He stood and held out his hand. "Come on, then. I'll help you move your things into another room."

She placed her fingers in his hand and he pulled her to her feet. She swayed slightly, from exhaustion or the wine, he wasn't sure. Will reached out to steady her and she leaned against him, her face pressed into his chest. "You're warm," she murmured. "Maybe I ought to put you in my room for the night and forget about a fire."

"I am warm," he replied. And growing warmer by the second. This physical contact between them was enough to stir his desire as evidenced by the blood racing to his groin.

Will wrapped his arms around her and gently rubbed her back. Her breathing grew soft and slow and he realized she was falling asleep in his arms. When her knees finally gave way, he reached down and scooped her off her feet.

Her eyes flew open and she cried out in surprise. "What are you doing?"

"I'm taking you up to your room," Will said, starting for the stairs. "You're nearly asleep and I'm not sure you can make it under your own power."

With a sigh, she settled into his grasp. "I think the service in this hotel is really wonderful," Claire said, resting her head against his shoulder. "I'm going to recommend it to all my friends."

Will took her to a room on the opposite end of the hall, kicking open the door with his foot. He'd placed a small space heater in the corner and had lit a fire in the fireplace and when they walked inside, the room was cozy. He hoped she wouldn't notice and that she'd repeat her invitation for him to stay and keep her warm.

He set her down next to the bed, her arms still wrapped around his neck. And when she turned her face up to his, he did what he'd wanted to do all evening. Will covered her mouth with his, savoring the taste of her. She responded without hesitation, her tongue meeting his, silently offering more than just a kiss.

The attraction between them was undeniable and intense, yet Will wasn't quite sure how to handle it. With any other woman, he wouldn't have hesitated to crawl into her bed and make love to her all night long. But Claire O'Connor was a guest! And then there was Sorcha's little love spell. If that had anything to do with this attraction, then Will wasn't about to let it affect his judgment.

Still, he couldn't resist enjoying just a few more moments with her. His hands skimmed over her body, slipping beneath the silk shirt to touch bare skin. She leaned closer, inviting further exploration, and there didn't seem to be anything standing in his way.

Will slowly worked at the buttons of her shirt, opening them one by one and bending to kiss each inch of exposed skin. When he reached the soft tops of her breasts, he sat down on the edge of the bed and pulled her into the space between his legs.

His lips found her belly, so smooth and warm, and he spanned her waist with his hands as he kissed her there. Claire ran her fingers through his hair, guiding his head until he reached the lacy fabric of her bra. Will nuzzled at the soft flesh, then reached up to tug the lace down to reveal her nipple.

Claire tipped her head back the instant his lips teased at the hard peak and a heartbeat later, they tumbled onto the bed in a tangle of limbs. All good sense seemed to vanish and Will focused on pleasure, the wonderful act of exploring her body with his lips and his fingers, inhaling her scent and listening to the tiny sounds that escaped from her throat with each tantalizing caress.

He twisted his fingers around hers and gently drew her arms above her head, gazing down into her face. "Are you sure you want this?"

She didn't open her eyes, but merely smiled. "Yes."

"Look at me," he said.

Claire opened her eyes and he stared down at her. "Would you like to go to sleep?" he asked.

"Yes," she replied.

Will rolled to his side, then stood next to the bed. If he was going to spend his pent-up passion on Claire O'Connor, then it was going to be a night both of them remembered, a night that went on far longer than the next hour or two. He reached down and drew the covers back.

"You're going to thank me for this tomorrow morning," he muttered as he took off her shoes. "Don't get me wrong. I enjoy a good roll in the sack, but I can control my impulses. Not that it isn't killing me to walk out of this room." Will carefully rebuttoned her shirt. "I sure won't be getting any sleep tonight."

He pulled the bedcovers up over her and tucked them under her chin, then bent down and brushed a kiss onto her lips. "We'll take this up another time," he said.

"Another time," she whispered, a tiny smile curling her lips.

He walked out of the room, closing the door behind him, then made his way through the quiet hallway to the stairs. On his way through the parlor, he grabbed the wineglasses and empty bottle before heading back to the kitchen.

Though it was late, he wasn't tired. In truth, he was so wound up, he wondered if he'd sleep at all. Or if he'd spend the entire night thinking about the beautiful woman in room three, knowing she was just upstairs, knowing that if he really wanted to, he could walk into her room and crawl into her bed. He'd been invited.

"Was she wild for you?"

Will spun around to see Sorcha standing in the doorway. She was dressed in a long white robe with a jeweled belt cinched at the waist and a wreath of holly leaves on her head. "Jaysus, what the hell are you doing here?"

"I was curious," she said, crossing the room to stand in front of him. "I wanted to see if my spell worked."

"No," he lied. "Did you really expect that it would?"

She frowned, staring into his face as if she could read his mind. "Why don't you believe in my powers, Will? They're real, you know."

"Sorcha, it's late and I need to get some sleep. Go home."

"I can't. I have to go out to the stone circle and do an incantation. Maggie Foley wants grandchildren and she's paying me for a weekly fertility ritual on behalf of her three daughters."

"But you'd rather come here and bother me?"

"If you don't believe in the magic, it won't work." She reached into her bag and withdrew an old bottle, stopped with a cork. "Here, you might as well have this. You need all the help you can find."

"What is it?"

"Water from the Druid spring. Use it. If you don't have a woman soon, I think you're going to go right round the bend. It's not good for a man to have all that unreleased sexual energy. It's not healthy."

"I blame that on you and every other person who lives on Trall. You were the eedjits who put my name up for that bachelor story. Thought it might bring more publicity to Trall. Well, it didn't. But it ruined my social life."

"The water could change all that," Sorcha said.

"There is no Druid spring," Will countered. "You probably drew this water right from the tap at your flat." He pulled out the stopper and dumped the water into the sink, then handed her the empty bottle.

She shrugged. "All right. Suit yourself." Sorcha turned for the door.

"Are you going to remove the spell?" Will called.

She slowly faced him again, a satisfied grin curling her lips. "You do believe, you just can't admit it. My work here is done. The rest is up to you."

With that, she spun around, her robes billowing out as she left the room. Will chuckled to himself. So maybe there was something to Sorcha's spell. He'd give Claire tonight to sleep off her jet lag and the wine they'd drunk. But tomorrow, he'd get down to the bottom of this crazy attraction between them. And then he'd know for sure if Sorcha's Druid powers had any effect on him at all.

CLAIRE SLOWLY came awake, opening her eyes to the soft sunlight in the room. At first, she wasn't sure where she was. She closed her eyes again, certain she was dreaming, but then realized she wasn't asleep. Pushing up on her elbow, she looked around the unfamiliar room. It wasn't her bedroom—but then, she was in Ireland, wasn't she? But this wasn't the room she'd been put in, either. Her luggage wasn't anywhere to be seen. Slowly, the events of the previous night came back to her.

"Oh, no," she murmured. Was this *his* room? Had they spent the night together in *his* bed? Wincing, she sat up and peeked under the covers. A sigh of relief escaped her lips. She was still dressed, though her blouse wasn't buttoned right. "I didn't do anything stupid." Claire frowned. "Why didn't I do anything stupid?"

A soft knock sounded on the door and Claire crawled out of bed. She smoothed the wrinkles in her shirt and ran a hand through her hair before she opened the door. Will stood on the other side with a tray. "I made you some coffee," he said. "I thought you might need it."

Claire rubbed her temple, suddenly aware of the ache there. "What time is it?"

"Noon," he said. "Which is about six a.m. Chicago time. I can bring the coffee back later, if you like. Your bags are out here in the hall."

Claire stepped away from the door and motioned him inside. She sat down on the edge of the bed and he placed the tray on a small table and set it in front of her. Then he poured her a mug of coffee. "There's milk and sugar," he said, pointing to the tray.

"Black is fine." She took a sip, watching him over the rim of the mug. "What happened last night?"

"You don't remember?"

"Parts of it are a little hazy. I didn't have that much to drink. Just a few glasses of wine."

He walked out the door and returned with her luggage, setting the bags at the foot of the bed. "I think you were more tired than drunk," Will said. "You got sleepy and I brought you up here and—"

"And?"

"And put you to bed."

"That's all?" Claire asked.

"Yes," he said. "Well, not entirely. We did mess around a bit before you fell asleep."

"Define messing around," Claire said. "I don't want to mistranslate here."

Will reached out and took her hand, toying with her fingers as he spoke. "We kissed and touched and that was about the end of it. And you invited me to spend the night, but I didn't want to take advantage."

"That was noble of you," she said.

"Not that noble. Believe me, I considered taking you up on your offer. I spent most of last night kicking my own arse because I hadn't. I live on a damned island. Beautiful women don't come along every day."

"I'm sorry," Claire said.

"For what?"

"Leading you on. I—I really didn't come here for—Well, even though I find you very—" Claire quickly took another sip of her coffee. Why was she having such a difficult time telling him she didn't want him? Claire groaned inwardly. Maybe because she wanted Will Donovan more than she'd ever wanted a man before?

"You came here for a vacation," Will said. He slowly stood. "If you'd like, I'll take you out today and show you some of the sights."

"Thank you. But I thought I'd walk into town and do a little shopping."

"Well, be sure to put on something warm. There's a chill in the air."

Claire watched as he walked out of the room, closing the door behind him. She let out a tightly held breath, then flopped back on the bed. In truth, she would have been perfectly happy to spend the entire day with Will, curled up in front of a blazing fire, sipping wine, getting to know each other…more intimately. But she'd come to Trall specifically to find the Druid spring. And if she hoped to accomplish her goal, then she'd have to do some investigative work. And the first person she'd go to see was that Druid priestess that Captain Billy mentioned. If anyone knew about the Druid spring, she would.

When she'd finished her coffee, Claire unpacked. She followed Will's advice and picked out a warm wool sweater and a pair of corduroy pants. Then she brushed her teeth and ran a comb through her hair, deciding to forgo makeup. There was no use attracting unwarranted attention from the innkeeper.

She found Will sitting at the dining room table, a pile of papers spread out in front of him. She watched him, unseen, from the doorway, admiring the handsome features of his face, the strong set of his jaw and the sensuous mouth.

His hair was thick, an indistinct color somewhere between brown and black, and long enough to brush against his collar. Her fingers twitched as she recalled the feel of it. His profile was almost aristocratic, a perfectly straight nose, a high forehead, a strong chin. She'd always thought Eric the most handsome man she'd ever met, but he seemed rather ordinary compared to Will.

So how had a man like Will remained unattached? Surely, one of Ireland's most eligible bachelors had had his choice of available females. He had a charming personality; he was good-looking, polite, with just a hint of bad boy thrown in. And he'd managed to nearly seduce her, a complete stranger, without even trying. Surely there was one attractive, single woman in all of Ireland who'd wanted him for her own.

Claire cleared her throat as she walked into the room

and Will glanced up. He slowly stood, his gaze fixed on her. "Hi," he said.

"I'm sorry to interrupt," Claire said. "I hoped that you might give me some information."

"About?"

"The captain of the mail boat was telling me about a Druid princess—no, priestess—who lives on the island. I'd like to meet her."

Will was silent for a long moment. "You want to meet Sorcha? Why?"

"I don't know. She sounds…interesting. Does she have a shop in town?"

Will nodded. "It's called The Dragon's Heart. She makes jewelry and little Druid trinkets. But, she's really a bit—" He paused. "Eccentric. She sometimes has a tendency to promise more than she can deliver. If you'd like to see her, I could take you."

"No, I'm just curious. What else would you suggest? I thought I might make a list to be sure I saw everything before I left."

Will chuckled. "You don't need a list. There's not that much to see. There's the church. There are some beautiful relics inside and some interesting Celtic crosses in the graveyard. There's a small museum about the island just back of the post office. And there are some lovely shops along Parsons Street, antiques and such. There's a tour of the island that leaves at noon from the market square in a horse-drawn carriage. Most of the tourists enjoy that."

"And what about the things you find interesting?" she asked.

"There's the stone circle," Will said.

"Like Stonehenge?"

"Not nearly as grand. But interesting. I can take you if you'd like. I'm finished here. And after we go, we can stop in town for lunch."

Claire considered his invitation, then nodded. What harm could it do? Despite wanting to keep her distance, spending the day with Will would be infinitely more interesting than wandering about the island on her own. And in the light of day she could certainly control her impulses around him. "All right," she said.

He held out his hand and she hesitantly placed hers in his. The instant she touched him, Claire regretted accepting his offer. His fingers were warm and strong and she imagined them skimming over her naked skin, raking through her hair, touching her in places far too intimate to contemplate. She tugged her hand away and fumbled with the buttons of her jacket.

"I just need to grab a coat and we can go," Will said.

They walked out the kitchen door to the carriage house. Will helped her into a Range Rover, then circled around and got in the driver's side. As they bumped down the lane, Claire risked a glance over at him. She smiled to herself. She could look, but touching was a bad idea. Looking couldn't possibly get her in trouble, could it?

They drove away from the village, winding around through the barren, windswept hillsides at the center of the island. Once, they had to stop and wait for a flock of sheep to meander across the road. Will pointed out the old stone cottages along the way and the remains of a castle keep that was now nothing more than a pile of rocks.

They came to the crest of a hill and a moment later,

Claire could see the ocean again. Will pulled the Range Rover to a stop. "We'll have to walk from here," he said. "It's not far."

She jumped out of the truck and joined him as he started off down a small footpath. He held her hand for most of the way and when the path grew rocky, he walked in front, turning to help her climb over stone fences, his hands firm on her waist as she made her way between rickety wood stiles. They trudged over another small rise and suddenly, a wide, lush green meadow appeared before them, the circle of pillars rising toward the sky.

Claire's breath caught in her throat. "It's beautiful," she murmured.

Will turned to her and looked down into her eyes. He reached out, brushing his fingertips over her cheek, and Claire shivered at his touch. She waited, unsure of how to react, her breath coming in tiny gasps that made her a bit dizzy.

And then, he bent closer and kissed her, his mouth warm on hers. Claire parted her lips as the kiss deepened and she felt her mind spinning with desire and her body pulsing with wonderful sensations. But then the kiss ended as suddenly as it had begun.

Will glanced up at the sky. "We'd better hurry along. It looks like it's going to rain."

They walked down the steep hill to the circle of rough pillars. It was like a miniature version of Stonehenge, the stones no more than ten feet high and four feet wide. The diameter of the circle was at least fifty or sixty feet.

She slowly walked around the outside, touching each

pillar as she passed it, surprised by the strange atmosphere. She could feel the magic all around them, like electricity in the air or a scent in the wind.

"It's very powerful," she said. "What did they do here?"

Will shrugged. "They say it's like a calendar. The Druids celebrated at specific times of the year. At both solstices and both equinoxes. Beltane and Samhain and a couple others I can't remember. In fact, Sorcha does her Samhain celebration on Friday, if you'll still be here. The whole island comes to watch. It's all very pagan."

"Did they do sacrifices?"

"Like virgins?" He chuckled. "When I was a teenager we used to come out here with girls. We thought the magic would help us get lucky."

"Did it work?" Claire asked.

"Sometimes. I felt a girl up for the first time right over there. I thought I was doing all right."

"And do you ever come out here with women now?"

"I'm here with you," Will said with devilish grin.

Claire chuckled. "And do you expect to get lucky with me?"

Will grabbed her by the waist and drew her over to one of the stones, trapping her against it with his arms. He pressed his hips against hers and stared down into her eyes. "Times have changed. Maybe you should get lucky with me." He turned her around until he leaned back against the pillar, her hands now braced on either side of his hips.

"Will you let me get to first base?" Claire teased.

He frowned. "First base? As in, baseball?"

"Yes," she said.

"You played baseball?"

Claire shook her head. "No. It's just a way of saying how far you went with a boy. Actually, boys use it to discuss their prowess with girls. First base is kissing. Second base is hands under the shirt. Third base is hands in the pants and a home run is full-on sex."

"No wonder Americans are so fond of baseball," he said. "Much more interesting than cricket. So we've been to second base, then," Will said.

"We have?"

"Last night," he said. "There was some groping that went on." He reached down and slipped his hand beneath her sweater, finding the warm skin beneath.

Claire shivered at his touch, then mimicked his caress, slipping her hand under his sweater and sliding her palm up his chest. "Yes, I suppose you could consider this second base."

He cupped her lace-covered breast in his palm and ran his thumb over her nipple, drawing it to a peak. Claire sighed softly and closed her eyes and a moment later, his lips met hers in a deep, demanding kiss.

Suddenly, she couldn't stop touching him. She shoved him against the pillar and pushed his sweater up, revealing the muscled flesh of his abdomen. Impatient, Will shrugged out of his jacket, then yanked his sweater and T-shirt over his head. The brisk wind caused goosebumps on his skin and Claire pressed her lips to his chest. She was still fully clothed and he'd made no move to undress her, his hand still hidden beneath her own sweater.

Slowly, she drew her tongue to his nipple, then

circled it several times. It grew to a hard peak under her ministrations and Claire continued to tease at it. He groaned softly, and ran his fingers through her hair, tangling in the windblown strands.

Her hands drifted down his to belt and then lower, smoothing over the fabric of his jeans until she felt his growing erection beneath. Normally, she might have hesitated. But this mystical place made her feel bold and uninhibited, as if they'd stepped into another world where there were no rules, only impulses and desires.

Claire began to work at his belt while Will leaned back against the stone pillar. He watched her as she fumbled with the buckle, holding his breath as if her touch were enough to send him over the edge. Claire had nearly got it unfastened when she felt the first drop of rain hit her head.

A moment later, the skies opened up. She glanced up at Will to see him smiling…and shivering. "I guess the gods have spoken," he said.

Claire giggled, then reached down and handed him his sweater. "Should we listen to them?"

"Just until we find someplace out of the rain." Will grabbed his jacket and they ran toward the path, the downpour soaking them both. But Claire didn't care. She'd never experienced anything quite so exciting as this. There was something between them, some force of nature, that couldn't be denied.

Was it part of this magical place or part of this land? Where did these feelings come from? And why did she feel so compelled to act upon them? For a moment, she thought about stopping him, about lying down in the soft, wet grass and making love right here in the middle of the meadow.

But in the end, she decided that a warm bed and a crackling fire would be much more conducive to an afternoon of pleasure. And the only place to find that was back at the inn.

"I REALLY DON'T THINK it's broken."

Will reached out and gently pushed Claire's jacket sleeve up to examine her wrist. On the way back to the Range Rover, Claire had slipped on a moss-covered rock and gone down hard. She now lay sprawled in a muddy patch of the footpath, her hair drenched, her clothes dirty.

"Wiggle your fingers," he said. She winced as she did and Will sat back on his heels. "I think it may be broken."

"It's probably just a sprain," Claire insisted. "Really. Just help me up. It'll feel better once I put some ice on it."

Will tugged his jumper over his head and fashioned a crude sling, then slipped into his jacket. He carefully helped her back to the car and once he'd settled her inside, got behind the wheel. As they drove the short distance back to the inn, Will glanced over at her. She was trying to make light of the accident, but it was clear from the tight set of her jaw she was in considerable pain.

Claire met his gaze and forced a smile. "It's already feeling better," she assured him.

Will turned his attention back to the road, navigating the bumps and soggy parts as carefully as he could.

But every time the Range Rover took a hard bounce, Claire let out a tiny cry of pain.

When they reached the main road, he turned toward the village. "We've got a medical clinic here on the island." She opened her mouth to protest, but he reached out and put his finger over her lips. "Humor me."

Will reached into his jacket pocket for his mobile and rang up Annie Mulroony, the nurse who staffed the clinic on a daily basis, and Sorcha's mother. "The doctor comes over from the mainland once a week," he explained to Claire. "If we're lucky, he'll be in today."

Five minutes later, they arrived at the small, whitewashed cottage on the edge of the village. Annie was waiting at the door. She'd been the island's nurse and midwife for the last twenty-five years and had patched up all manner of minor injuries and seen to the births of most everyone under the age of twenty. The patients she couldn't handle were sent to the mainland, the serious by helicopter and the rest by the ferry.

"What seems to be the problem, then?" she asked as she helped Claire into the surgery.

"I think it's just bruised," Claire said.

Annie glanced over at Will as she settled Claire onto the examining table. "And where were you two mucking about? You look like you just crawled out of the sea."

"I took her over to the stone circle," Will replied. "She slipped on the path and fell."

Annie gave him a disapproving frown. "You know what comes of that business. The gods don't like it when you desecrate their holy place with hanky-panky."

"We were just sightseeing," Will said.

Annie glanced back to Claire. "Is that true, lass?" A flush of pink stained Claire's cheeks and Annie shook her head. "I see. Well, let's have an X ray of this, shall we? If it's broken, we'll splint it and wait for the doctor to put on a cast. He'll be here tomorrow." She glanced over her shoulder to Will. "Young man, you may wait outside."

Will found a chair in the reception room and distractedly flipped through a copy of *Hello!* magazine. But the celebrity gossip didn't occupy his interest and he got up and began to pace the width of the waiting area. He'd never believed in all the superstitions surrounding the stone circle. But Will had to wonder if perhaps he was being punished for taking advantage where he shouldn't have.

She was a guest, after all. And though she certainly had enjoyed what had gone on as much as he had, there was something slightly naughty about it as well. Hell, she'd made the first move with all her talk about baseball, so he had no reason to feel guilty.

Fifteen minutes passed before Claire emerged from the examining room. Annie followed close behind. "She's fine," the nurse said, handing Will his jumper. "No broken bones that I can see, but I'll have a consult with Dr. Reilly tomorrow and if he finds anything, he'll ring you up. For the evening, keep ice on it and don't be turnin' any handsprings, dear."

"Thank you," Claire said. "And you'll send me the bill at the inn?"

"I'll take care of that," Will said. "Don't worry."

By the time they got back to the inn, Will could see Claire was in a considerable amount of discomfort. He walked her up to her room and then went back downstairs to change and fetch whatever pain medication he had on hand. When he got back to her room, he found her standing in front of the fireplace, struggling with the zipper on her pants.

"I can't get them off," she muttered, staring down at the mud-stained corduroy.

"Here, then, let me help." He tossed the bottles on the bed then crossed the room to stand in front of her. At first, Will wasn't sure how he ought to go about undressing Claire. In the end, he decided to try to remain as impassive as possible. He reached for the zipper and pulled it down, then slipped his palms beneath the waistband and skimmed the pants over her hips.

Will had undressed a fair number of women and had always enjoyed it. But the simple act of helping Claire out of her muddy clothes was charged with a current that made touching her electric.

He'd forgotten to remove her shoes and socks first, so he bent down and worked at the laces, grateful that he had something to turn his attention to besides her long, shapely legs...and the skimpy pair of panties she wore.

Claire picked up her foot, then lost her balance and swayed into him until the lace of her panties pressed against his chin. Will swallowed a groan and tried to ignore the activity going on inside his jeans. Maybe it would have been best to let her struggle on her own.

When he'd finally managed to yank off one shoe, he turned to the other. But when he grabbed Claire's ankle, she lost her balance completely and tumbled forward. Will wrapped his arms around her waist and softened her fall onto the carpet with his body. They lay together for a long moment in a tangle of limbs.

Claire stared down into his eyes, her pale hair tickling at his cheeks. Her pants were twisted around her ankles and Will was keenly aware of his arousal pressing between them. She shifted slightly, the silky fabric of her panties sliding against the front of his jeans.

A tiny smile teased at her lips as she deliberately moved against him. "What's that all about?" she whispered, tucking a strand of hair behind her ear.

"I was hoping you could tell me," Will replied. "You're the one who caused it."

"And am I responsible for getting rid of it?" she asked.

"Getting rid of it seems a bit harsh," Will said. "Maybe if we lie here for a moment we'll figure out how to make it go away."

Claire wrapped her good arm around his neck, then rolled off of him, pulling Will on top of her until their contact was even more intimate. Slowly, she began to move beneath him, in a tempting rhythm that did nothing to relieve his situation.

This was crazy, Will thought to himself. They'd only just met, yet there was an attraction between them, a desire that burned with greater intensity every time they touched. He closed his eyes, losing himself in the sensations coursing through his body. He'd enjoy it for just a moment and then, he'd do the sensible thing and leave the room.

But as he rocked against her, Will realized his need had completely overtaken his common sense. It felt good, as good as the first time he'd experienced it as a teenager, this overwhelming need for release at any cost.

Will furrowed his fingers through her hair and kissed her, gently at first, then more desperately as his desire became more acute. She was beautiful and exciting and irresistible and he couldn't seem to get enough of her. But she was also a complete stranger and a guest in his inn.

He drew a deep breath and stopped, then rolled off of her. Covering his eyes with his arm, Will moaned. "This is crazy. We have to stop this." It was Sorcha's fault. She'd put all these ideas into his head and now he was acting on them.

Claire sat up and brushed the hair out of her eyes, then kicked off her pants. "I didn't start it," she murmured.

A laugh escaped his throat. "Yes, you did. What's that all about? That's what you said."

"I was asking a question." She tossed her muddy pants into the corner, then stood and yanked off her jumper, throwing that aside as well. She stood over him in just a T-shirt and her underwear. "I think I'll take a bath."

"Are you resolved to torture me?" Will asked, staring up at her.

She studied him for a long moment, then shook her head. "I have no idea what I'm doing. As soon as I do, I'll let you know."

With that, Claire walked into the bathroom and shut the door behind her. A few moments later, Will heard the water hit the tub. He closed his eyes again and imagined her stripping off the remainder of her clothes and stepping into the warm water.

Once Claire had settled in for the evening, he'd find Sorcha straight away and insist that she remove whatever spells were still pending. How the hell was he supposed to resist this woman when she did absolutely nothing to resist him? Sorcha would fix it. And after that, he'd certainly be able to control this desperate need he had to seduce Claire O'Connor.

3

WHEN SHE EMERGED from the bathroom, wrapped in a towel, Claire found a fire crackling in the fireplace. She stood at the mantel and held her palms out to the warmth. To her relief, Will had decided to use her bath as an excuse to leave the room.

She ran her hand through her damp hair, then grabbed her robe and slipped it on. Since the moment she'd arrived at the inn, all her thoughts had been focused on the handsome innkeeper. It was like she'd stepped into some fantasy world, where men and women were instantly attracted…and willing to throw themselves into each other's arms without thinking.

But she'd always carefully considered every step in a romantic relationship. Claire O'Connor was nothing if not prudent. And going to bed with a man she'd only just met twenty-four hours before was the epitome of… "Stupidity," she muttered to herself.

Yes, she was in a foreign land and all her troubles did seem oceans away. And staring into Will Donovan's beautiful eyes did have an amnesia-like effect on her. Staying in Ireland for the next month to let a love affair play out between her and Will Donovan was just not an option. Eric was her future and it was time to get down to business, time to find the Druid spring, get a bottle of water and go home.

She opened the top drawer of the dresser and pulled out the tattered, velvet-covered journal. She still occasionally jotted down important thoughts and reminders, but whenever she felt her world shifting on its axis, she went back to the journal, to the plan she'd made for her life.

Claire flipped through the pages. There was the list of her top ten colleges. She'd attended her number one—Northwestern—on a partial scholarship. And then there was the list of boys she'd wanted to take her to prom. Again, she'd gone with the first boy on her list, although three through six had asked her as well.

She found the page headed My Future Husband and scanned the list. "One, he must be handsome. Two, he must have dark hair and beautiful eyes. Three, he must love Madonna." All right, that one didn't matter. "He must be successful. He must live in Chicago. He must love cats." Claire continued to go through the list, recalling the moment she'd realized that Eric met all her criteria, including a fondness for Madonna. She'd even cut out a photo from a magazine and pasted it in her journal, and Eric had borne a slight resemblance to the man in the photo.

Claire paged through the book until she found the photo. The moment she looked at it, her breath caught in her throat. There was something familiar in the eyes, something that looked remarkably like—Will Donovan.

She quickly closed the book and put it back into its

spot beneath her underwear. So maybe Will did fit a few of her criteria, but all her plans had been built around Eric. So why was she so tempted by Will?

She'd never in her life thrown herself into a purely sexual affair, never experienced that kind of physical excitement. And though her practical side wanted to listen to all the warning bells, another part of her wanted to throw caution to the wind. And if she ever wanted to let loose, then Will Donovan was probably her best bet.

After all, she could make every wild fantasy come true here in Ireland and then she could hop on a plane and go back to her real life, with no regrets. Perhaps she owed it to herself to explore that side of her nature, the side she kept so well-hidden. She planned to marry Eric and after the wedding, there'd be no second chances.

A soft knock sounded on the door and Claire ran her fingers through her damp hair. "Come in," she said, clutching her robe together over her breasts.

The door slowly swung open and Will stood on the other side. "I've made some supper," he said. "It's down in the kitchen. I have to go out but I'll be back later. If you're hungry, just help yourself."

Claire forced a smile and tried to ignore her racing pulse. How was it possible that this man had such an effect on her? Was it the way he stared at her, always looking so deeply into her eyes that it felt as though he were undressing her soul as well as her body? Or was it the way his mouth seemed to be a heartbeat away from kissing hers? A shiver skittered down her spine and she took a step back and turned her attention to the fire. "Thanks for the fire," she murmured. "And the offer of dinner. But I'm really not very hungry."

"It's there if you want it," he said. "I mean the food. Supper. In the kitchen."

"I know what you meant," Claire said, glancing over at him.

"I'll just be off, then. I shouldn't be long."

Claire kept her gaze fixed on the fire until she heard the door click shut, then groaned softly. Cradling her wrist, she fell backwards onto the bed, then pinched her eyes closed and tried to put every last thought of Will Donovan out of her head. She rolled off the bed and walked to the windows, which overlooked the front drive.

Drawing back the lacy curtain, Claire watched as Will strode out to the Range Rover. Gravel sprayed from beneath the tires as he sped away. Whatever the errand, he was obviously in a hurry.

Claire spent the next half hour wandering around her room and trying to convince herself that she hadn't made a mistake in coming to Ireland. Though it had taken a major portion of her savings just to buy the plane ticket on such short notice, at the time the expense had seemed well worth it. But the more she thought about the Druid spring and the silly legend behind it, the more she began to feel like a fool.

She'd always been so sure of what she'd wanted. And now, the very first time her life plan had hit a bump in the road, she'd gone off on some silly quest for magic water. Her stomach rumbled and Claire closed her eyes. She hadn't eaten since lunch and it was nearly nine. And it would be better to visit the kitchen now, while Will was out and about, than risk running into him.

She walked out of the room and down the stairs, the thick carpet soft against her bare feet. The lights were low and when she got to the kitchen, she found the room illuminated only by a small light above the sink.

A pot of stew simmered on the stove and a loaf of crusty bread sat waiting on a cutting board. Claire grabbed a glass from the dish drainer, then opened the refrigerator to find something to drink. She sniffed at a carton of milk, then filled her glass, and returned the carton to the fridge.

"You must be the American."

The voice came out of the darkness and Claire spun around, the milk sloshing out of the glass as she moved. A slender figure, draped in a white robe, emerged from the shadows near the back door.

The woman had flame-red hair, tangled in waves around her pale face, and a smudge of what looked like soot on her forehead. "You frightened me," Claire murmured, pressing her hand to her chest.

"Sorry," she said with an apologetic smile. "You ought to try the stew. Will makes a fine lamb stew."

"He's not here," Claire said. "He went out on some errand."

"I know. He's looking for me. I'm avoiding him."

A tiny sliver of jealousy shot through her. Was this woman Will's lover? She certainly was beautiful. "I see," Claire said, nodding her head.

"Oh, not in the way you think. Will and I are friends. I suppose you could call me his spiritual adviser?" She held out her hand. "I'm Sorcha Mulroony."

"Oh, you're the Druid princess."

"Priestess. Or sorceress if you must. Princesses have such awful reputations."

Claire reached out and shook her hand. "Claire O'Connor. The American."

"You are lovely," Sorcha said, studying her. "Lucky that, considering Will's rather lengthy dry spell. We were lovers once, you know. But no more."

"I—I see."

"It's been a long time, so not to worry." Sorcha took the glass of milk from Claire's hand, then jumped up to sit on the edge of the counter, her muddy bare feet swinging from beneath her robe. "So have you seduced him yet? He's quite wonderful in bed. Very…intense." She took a sip of the milk, watching Claire over the rim of the glass.

Claire tried to cover her surprise at the audacious question. "Why would you think I'd seduce him?"

Sorcha reached behind her and grabbed a covered crock, then removed a cookie and began to nibble it. "You aren't married, are you?"

"No."

"Engaged?"

Sorcha handed Claire a cookie. Claire opened her mouth to reply in the affirmative, then realized it would be a lie. "Not really. Not yet."

"Well, then, why on earth wouldn't you? You owe it to yourself to explore your primal urges. I'm all about primal urges. If you'd like, I could cast a spell. For a hundred euros I could make you irresistible to him." She took another bite of the cookie. "I also take credit cards." Sorcha studied her for a moment, then shook her head. "Don't look so shocked. A girl has to do what a girl has to do to have a bit of fun now and then, don't you agree?"

Claire set the cookie on the counter, trying to find the right words to frame her question. "Have you ever heard of the Druid spring? My grandmother told me that there's a spring on this island that has magic water."

"Of course," she said. "I know where it is."

"Could you show me?" Claire asked.

Sorcha frowned. "It's a professional secret."

"I could pay you," Claire offered.

"First you'd have to tell me why you'd want the water," Sorcha said. "And then I might consider it." She hopped to the floor and wandered to the back door. "We'll talk later. I better leave before Will gets back. Samhain is the night after tomorrow. I'm swamped until the day after. I promise, we'll chat then. We'll do lunch, won't that be fun?"

"Wait," Claire called. "I'm supposed to leave tomorrow."

"No, you aren't. Consider what I've said." Sorcha reached for the door. "A chance like this doesn't come about every day." A chilly breeze billowed her robes as she stepped outside.

Claire ran to the door and watched as the priestess disappeared into the dark night. "Intense," she whispered. When was the last time she had sex that even came close to being intense? Never. "What happens in Ireland stays in Ireland," she said, turning away from the door.

Tomorrow, she'd go into town and do her best to find

the location of the Druid spring. With any luck, she'd get what she came for and be on her way back home before week's end. But as she slowly walked up the stairs to her room with a handful of cookies and a glass of milk, Claire couldn't help but wonder if she might come to regret a hasty departure.

After all, despite her wishing otherwise, she and Eric were officially over. Why not enjoy another man's company and stick a toe in that great whirlpool known as sexual desire? "Why not?" she muttered. "Because I've never been much of a swimmer and might just get sucked in and drown."

But then, drowning in a vortex of hot sex wouldn't be the worst way to go, would it?

WILL WAVED to the barman as he entered the pub, then wove his way through the rough wooden tables at the Jolly Farmer. The air was thick with smoke and the floor sticky with spilt ale. "I'm looking for Sorcha," he said, leaning over to speak to Dennis Fraser. "Have you seen her?"

Dennis nodded in the direction of the rear of the pub and, through the haze, Will caught sight of Sorcha, sitting at a table with two of the village's elderly residents. He strode to her table, then stood over it until she looked up. "I've been all over the island looking for you," he said. "We need to talk."

"So I've heard. I'm in the middle of a consultation here," she replied. "Mr. Kelly would like to know when to expect a frost and Mr. Kearney is worried about his prospects for winning the Lotto."

Will reached out and grabbed Sorcha's hand, then pulled her to her feet. "Gentlemen, she'll be back straightaway," he said. He dragged her toward the door and out onto the cobblestone street.

"What's got you all bothered?" Sorcha asked.

"Take the bloody spell off," he said. "Right now. Do it or you and I are no longer friends."

Sorcha frowned. "That sounds like a threat. Are you threatening me, Will Donovan?"

"Just do it. Am I clear?"

Sorcha put on a pout, then nodded. "Although I can't understand why. She's quite lovely, Will, and I have no doubt that with a bit of coaxing she'd find your bed very comfortable. We had a chat and I do believe she is quite open to the prospect of—"

"You spoke to her?"

Sorcha nodded. "I stopped by the inn. I heard you were looking for me. We had a lovely little talk, just us girls, and I was very flattering about your sexual prowess. You would have been proud of me."

Will ground his teeth, trying to keep his temper in check. God, the worst thing about living on this feckin' island was having everyone sticking their nose into his personal life. "Sorcha, make it happen. Tonight."

With that, he turned and walked toward the Range Rover, cursing beneath his breath. Hell, he'd never believed in her damn magic, but there was no other way to explain this wild sexual attraction to Claire O'Connor.

Jaysus, Mary and Joseph, with Sorcha's meddling, he might as well have his mother living with him with her incessant questions about settling down and raising a family. The only person who ought to care about his sex life—or lack of—should be him.

By the time he drove the short distance to the inn, he'd managed to calm his anger and frustration. It was nearly midnight and he'd had a long day. A whiskey, a warm bed and a good, hard sleep was all he wanted. Tomorrow morning, he'd wake up a new man.

Yet as he walked through the back door into the kitchen, Will's thoughts immediately went to the guest upstairs. His only guest. Though November had always been slow for tourists on the island, he was almost hoping that one or two might show up and give him something to occupy his time—and his mind.

He walked through the darkened kitchen, shrugging out of his jacket and tossing it over a stool. The lights were still burning in the front parlor and he turned them off, before walking to his room at the back of the inn. But as he passed the stairway, Will couldn't resist checking up on Claire.

As he rounded the corner to the upstairs hall, he noticed light from her room spilling out onto the carpet. He hesitated, at first thinking it better to turn around and go back to his own room. But then, curiosity got the better of him and he continued on. He stepped into the open doorway and found Claire curled up in one of the overstuffed chairs she'd dragged to a spot near the fireplace. Her feet were tucked beneath her and an open book rested on her lap. Their gazes met for a long moment.

"I didn't expect you'd still be awake," he said softly, bracing his arm on the doorjamb.

"I couldn't sleep. Every time I tried, I'd roll over on my wrist and wake myself up."

"Can I get you anything?"

She nodded. "I wouldn't mind a cup of tea if it's not too much trouble."

"No trouble," he said.

She stood, dropping the book onto the chair. Her robe clung to the curves of her body like a second skin and Will knew she was naked underneath. His gaze drifted down to the tie neatly knotted at her waist and he wondered how long it might take to undo the knot and brush the silk garment aside.

"I—I'll get it," he said, his voiced choking as she moved closer.

"I thought I'd come with you," she said.

Claire moved to step around him and Will reached out to place his hands on her waist. He didn't think before he touched her, but the moment he did, he knew he was lost. Claire froze, staring up at him with wide, blue eyes. An instant later, his mouth captured hers and they tumbled onto the bed, taking up exactly where they'd left off earlier.

He was desperate to taste her again. He cupped her face in his hands and molded her mouth to his. Breathless, he trailed his lips along her neck, then drew her robe off her shoulder and nipped at the soft curve of her neck.

She smelled like the lavender bath soap the inn provided. On her, the scent was intoxicating, like a drug. His mouth found hers again and this time, he drew her into a slow, languid kiss, determined to take his time with her.

"Did you really have an errand to run?" she asked. "Or were you just trying to stay away from me?"

Will stared up at her, not certain how to reply. "Staying away from you seems to be a lost cause." He smoothed his hand over her face and dragged his thumb along her lower lip. "Would you like me to leave?"

She slid down along his body then began to unbutton his shirt, dropping soft kisses on each bit of skin as she revealed it. "No," Claire murmured.

"Did the ache in your arm really keep you awake or were you waiting for me?" Will asked.

"I couldn't sleep," she said, brushing his shirt aside. She sat up and straddled his hips. "My arm feels pretty good."

Will chuckled softly. He'd always hated the games that went on between men and women, the little lies, the silly flirtations, the endless advances and retreats. With Claire, it was different. They both seemed to want the same thing and weren't afraid to admit it.

He reached up and grabbed the front of her robe, tugging at the silk until he drew her back against his chest. "I want you to know that I don't do this with every guest who registers at the inn."

"Good to know," Claire said. She bit at his lower lip. "Although, I'm sure if you offered your services, you might have more guests in the off-season."

"Let me rephrase. I've never done this with a guest before."

This seemed to give her pause, and for a moment Will wondered if he'd said the wrong thing. "I guess there's a first time for everything," she intoned.

Will pulled her closer and nuzzled her neck,

kissing the warm spot beneath her ear. "How far do you want me to go?"

"I think a home run might be nice," Claire said.

With a low chuckle, Will rolled her over until she lay beside him. His hand slipped beneath the silky fabric of her robe to cup her breast and her breath caught as he began to caress her nipple. She was soft and perfect, every curve meant for his touch.

The more they kissed and touched, the more the need between them grew. They were in no hurry and, rather than undress, they simply pushed clothes aside. Buttons were undone, zippers lowered. Will's leg rested over her hip and Claire slipped her hand beneath the waistband of his jeans to rest in the small of his back.

There was only one moment when a tiny splinter of doubt crept in, one moment when he thought it might be best to run right back to first base and stay there for the duration of the game. But then, Claire's other hand smoothed over his chest and down his belly. She wrapped her fingers around his erection, rubbing him through the fabric of his boxers, slowly stroking until the last shred of indecision passed.

"I never had much appreciation for American games," he whispered, staring into her eyes. "But I could get to like this one."

He bunched the hem of her robe in his fist and drew it up along her hip, exposing the length of her leg to his touch. His fingers trailed along the inside of her thigh until her found the damp spot between her legs. Will touched her, slipping between the soft folds of her sex.

"Third base," she murmured, arching against him.

Will had always been one to enjoy the full spectrum of bedroom activities with a woman. Though foreplay was fun for a while, losing himself inside feminine flesh was the ultimate pleasure. But for now, with Claire, this was perfect, this slow, easy seduction.

He felt like a teenager, just discovering the wonders of a woman's body. With each caress, he learned how to read her desire, from her quickened breathing to her soft moans to the way she moved against his hand. And in turn, she learned what he needed from her.

Will didn't feel the urge to rush and he lingered over her body, kissing each new inch of skin that he revealed. His fingers worked at the knot in the tie to her robe and when he finally got it loose, he spread the front so that she lay naked to his eyes.

"You're beautiful," he murmured, his eyes drifting from her breasts to her toes and back again. He bent to run his tongue over her nipple and drew it to a hard peak. "And you taste good, too."

Claire giggled, then pushed against his shoulder until he lay on his back. She began at his collarbone, pressing a string of soft kisses down the center of his chest to his belly, her tongue leaving damp imprints on his skin. Will closed his eyes as he realized she was moving lower. A moment later, her lips closed around him and a wave of sensation coursed through his body.

He wasn't prepared for the flood of desire that overwhelmed him, the sheer shock of her damp mouth on his shaft. He opened his eyes and stared at the ceiling, trying to keep from losing himself in the first minute. If he watched her, he would be finished in seconds. She sensed his excitement and drew away, waiting until he was ready for more.

Will felt as if he were no longer in control of his need. With each stroke, she pulled him along toward the edge and then, when he was almost there, she drew him back. If there was a rule book for this game, then Claire knew it back to front, for she was doing everything in her power to prolong his pleasure. But even though her mouth brought him closer and closer, he wanted to share his release with her.

Gently, he drew her back into another kiss and together, they continued to touch each other. The pace quickened and she gasped as he found the exact spot to tease her. A tiny moan began in her throat and Will knew she was ready. Their gazes locked and he saw every wave of pleasure in her expression. Her need was a powerful stimulant to his own.

She whispered his name, once and then again, and he couldn't hold back any longer. But just as his orgasm wracked his body, Claire moaned, shuddering beside him as he exploded in her hand. Surge after surge of exquisite surrender followed and he tried to focus on the feel of her spasms against his fingers, in the pleasure he was giving her.

And when it was over, they lay side-by-side, breathless, sated, unable to move. Will wasn't sure what to say. He'd never experienced anything quite so powerful. His pulse began to slow and exhaustion robbed him of his ability to think.

He would worry about this tomorrow, he mused. But for now, he'd just enjoy the aftermath. Claire curled up against him and nuzzled her face into his shoulder. Reaching over her, he grabbed the blanket beneath them and pulled it around them both until they were cocooned in warmth. And then, Will closed his eyes and slept.

SUNLIGHT POURED through the window, pulling Claire from the drowsy depths of sleep. She squinted, then covered her eyes as they adjusted to the light. Her limbs were tangled in the bedclothes and she struggled to get free.

Unlike the morning before, she knew exactly where she was, and what she'd done the previous night. A tiny smile of satisfaction curved the corners of her mouth. She'd always told herself that sex didn't have to be wild and spontaneous in order to be great. But now that she'd actually experienced it for herself, Claire realized she'd been wrong. Wild and spontaneous was the best.

Like everything else in her life, sex, especially with Eric, had its place. She secretly scheduled it the same way she scheduled a manicure or an appointment with her personal trainer. She knew exactly how long Eric could wait in between appointments and planned accordingly.

But now, Claire realized that she'd just been going through the motions. What she and Will had shared last night was pure lust, the kind that made a girl forget all her inhibitions and fears. The kind that brought intense, toe-curling, mind-numbing pleasure.

"Intense," she murmured. She pushed up on her elbow and looked down into Will's face. At rest, he looked much younger, almost boyish. His hair curled at the ends, mussed by sleep. Claire reached out to finger a lock of it, remembering how it felt to furrow her hands through it as he kissed her.

The scruffy beard gave him a slightly dangerous look that made the contrasts between man and boy even more intriguing. Who was he? And why was he as attracted to her as she was to him? Maybe it was an Irish thing, she mused. Maybe he found her as unusual and exotic as she found him.

He did have the most beautiful eyes, a color she'd never seen before, an odd mix of gold and green, but not really hazel. She remembered how he'd watched her as they were both approaching their release, how he kept his gaze fixed on hers until the very last instant.

Her gaze drifted lower. His jeans were pushed down low on his hips, and she could see the outline of his penis through the thin fabric of his boxers. She reached out to touch him, but then pulled her hand back.

"Open your eyes," she whispered.

But Will was still deeply asleep, his arm thrown over his head, his naked chest rising and falling slowly with each breath he took. She carefully rolled off the bed and stood, then retied her silk robe.

A glance in the mirror above the fireplace brought a cry of dismay. She'd never been at her best in the morning, but this was awful. Her hair was a mess, her eyes were all puffy and her face had a deep wrinkle in one cheek from the pillow. Claire moved toward the bathroom, then heard a shout echo through the inn.

"Hello, there, is anyone about? Hello? We'd like to take room."

She glanced at the bed and then at the open door to the hallway. When she heard footsteps on the stairs, she panicked. Raking her fingers through her hair, she raced out into the hall and closed the door behind her. A moment later, an elderly couple appeared at the end of the hall.

"Hello, there," the man said. "Would you happen to be the innkeeper?"

"No," Claire said, clutching at her robe. "He's not downstairs?"

"He doesn't answer our calls. We've just come on the ferry. See, Glynis, I told you it was too early to check in."

"Well, George," the woman said, "it doesn't hurt to see if there's a room, does it?"

"He's probably just running an errand in town," Claire assured them. "I could take your name and give him the message."

"Would you know if he has a room available?"

Claire's first thought was to say no. She liked having Will all to herself. But he was trying to run a business and her selfishness shouldn't hurt his profits. "I—I'm not sure. I think he might have said that there was a big group coming in later this evening. You'd have to ask him."

"Hmm." The man glanced at his wife and shrugged. "Well, I suppose we could stop back later. We're going to take a stroll around the island. We're just in from Lincolnshire for the Samhain celebration tomorrow night. You're American, aren't you?"

"Yes," Claire said. "Just in from Chicago."

"Fine city, Chicago," Glynis said. "We were there—what was it, George, three or four years ago?"

"I believe it was five, dear. We went to the top of your Sears Tower. Quite the view."

"And we went to a very lovely shopping mall."

"Water Tower Place," Claire said.

"Yes, that was it. Well, it was a pleasure meeting you, dear. I think we'll just take one more look around for the innkeeper and then we'll be on our way."

Claire nodded and watched as they walked back down the hallway. As soon as they were out of sight, she slipped back into her room and jumped on the bed, shaking Will awake. "Will, get up."

He opened his eyes and frowned at her, but the expression was gradually replaced with a sleepy smile. "Good morning."

"There are some people here, downstairs, looking for a room. I talked to them in the hallway. They're down there looking for you."

He sat up and ran his fingers through his hair. "What time is it?"

"Eight, maybe nine. I—I told them—" She paused. "I said you were probably in town running errands."

Will grabbed her by the waist and pulled her back down on top of him. "Well done, you. That buys us some time. At least an hour or two."

"I—I also told them I thought the inn was booked for the night. You'd better go down and tell them I was wrong."

"Why should I?" he asked. "As far as I'm concerned, we can lock the front door and throw away the key. You're far too important a guest and you require my undivided attention."

"Will, I think it would be best if we—"

"Spend the rest of the day together," he said.

"Actually, I was thinking about walking into town. I met that Druid sorceress, Sorcha, last night and I thought I'd go and check out her shop. It sounded interesting."

"She mentioned she'd stopped by," Will said, his brow furrowed. "What did she tell you?"

Claire smiled. "She said you were once lovers but that was a long time ago. And she said that she can cast magic spells, for a price. We don't have Druids in Chicago—at least I don't think we do. And as long as I'm here, I'd like to check it out."

"It's all a fraud, you know. Sorcha pretends to have magical powers, but it's just a way to separate silly tourists from their money."

"I know. But I'm on vacation," Claire said. "And I really should contribute something to the local economy."

"Her shop won't be open. She's busy getting ready for her Samhain ceremony tomorrow night," he said. "I can take you into town. There's a tea shop near the library. They make the best raisin scones. We'll have some breakfast."

Claire shook her head. "I think I'd like to take some time for myself, if that's all right. I'm going to get dressed while you go back downstairs and see if you can catch up with George and Glynis from Lincolnshire."

Will gave her an odd look, a glint of suspicion in his eyes. "All right. But we will have supper together tonight. Promise me that much."

"Yes," Claire said. "Supper tonight."

He crawled out of bed and pulled up his jeans, then searched the room for his shirt. He found it at the foot of the bed and slipped into it. "I had an amazing time last night," he murmured as he worked at the buttons, his gaze fixed on her face.

Claire felt a blush warm her cheeks. "So did I."

He seemed satisfied then and nodded before he walked to the door. "Would you like breakfast?"

"I think I'll just grab an apple before I leave."

He reached into his pocket and handed her his keys. "Take the Range Rover. I've got another car I can use. I'll leave my mobile on the front seat. If you get lost or get in trouble, just hit one on the memory dial and it will ring the inn. I'll come and find you."

"It's an island. It's going to be a little difficult to get lost."

"Well, in case you need…anything," he said. He pulled open the door and stepped into the hallway. But at the last second, he reentered the room, grabbed her by the waist and kissed her, deeply and thoroughly. "I'll be downstairs."

Claire smiled. "Yes, I know."

When she was finally alone, she sat down on the edge of the bed. This had all happened so fast. And there was the risk that indulging in fantastic sex for the rest of her vacation might make it terribly difficult to leave. But Claire had no illusions that she and Will Donovan had a future together. After all, he lived on an island an ocean away from Chicago. And she had a fiancé back in the States.

Claire groaned. No, she didn't, did she? And what

did Eric really mean to her after all? With every day she spent on this island, he seemed to fade further from her thoughts, replaced by fantasies of Will Donovan. But was she willing to give up on a three-year relationship for a vacation fling?

She quickly threw on the warmest clothes she could find and went downstairs. Will was in the kitchen, engrossed in the newspaper. She grabbed an apple from the bowl on the counter, promised him she'd be back before dinner, then indulged in a very long, passionate goodbye kiss. Will did his best to convince her to take him along, but Claire was adamant. She needed to find that spring and she wasn't willing to explain her determination to him.

Driving the Range Rover was a bit unnerving with the steering wheel on the opposite side. But she kept reminding herself to keep her side of the truck on the centerline and she'd be fine. She carefully navigated the narrow cobblestone streets of the village and then decided to take the first parking space she could find and walk.

She found Sorcha's shop easily, an ornately carved dragon on the sign above the door. Even though Will had told her the shop would be closed, she tried the door. Locked. She peered through the windows but couldn't see anything in the dark interior.

"She's out at the stone circle," a voice called.

Claire spun around to see the village nurse, Annie Mulroony, approach, lugging two canvas shopping bags. Her white hair was mussed by the damp breeze and she looked as though she were about to drop. "Can I help you with those?" Claire offered.

"No, no. My car is just there on the street," she said, nodding at a battered sedan parked on the opposite side. "How is your wrist? Better, I hope."

"Much better," Claire said, holding her hand up and wiggling her fingers. "Hardly any pain."

"Sorcha is getting ready for Samhain. She does a big show out at the stone circle. Tomorrow night at eight. Everyone goes. There's dancing and chanting and bonfires."

"I was hoping to visit her shop."

"I'm sure she'll be back before supper." Annie paused. "How has your stay been so far? I hope Will is treating you well."

"Yes, he is."

"Our Will, he's quite the handsome lad, don't you think?"

Claire glanced around uneasily. Did everyone on the island know what had happened between them last night? Or was she just imagining things? "Yes, he is."

"He's a fine catch for some young lady. I once thought he and Sorcha might be a match, but Sorcha is a bit…temperamental. He's well-off, you know. Though he doesn't look it."

"Really?"

Annie leaned nearer. "I don't like to gossip and it really isn't gossip since it's been published in the papers, but he's worth millions."

"Will? From the inn?"

"He invented some computer program. He had a company in Killarney and sold it right before he came back to the island. I think he's hiding out here. All those women chasing after him. It must have been very tiresome."

Claire nodded, uncomfortable with the subject of their chat. If Will had so many women lusting after him, what was he doing with her? Was she just another notch in his bedpost? Claire caught sight of a sign for the village's library. "I think I'll stop by again later." She gave Annie a wave and continued down the street to a small, white-washed cottage set right on the walkway. This time when she tried the door, it opened.

She stepped inside and glanced around. Books lined every wall, stacked from floor to ceiling and stuffed in every possible nook and cranny. She walked along the fiction section and then moved into self-help. But it took her a few minutes to find what she was looking for.

"Local history," she said as she grabbed a book on the island from the shelf and flipped through it. There had to be something in some book about the Druid spring.

"Can I help you find somethin'?" A plump red-haired woman entered the room, wiping her hands on an apron. "I was just fixing myself a pot of tea. Would you care to— Ah, you're the American. Claire, is it? I'm Beatrice Fraser."

"Yes, I'm Claire. Claire O'Connor. The American. Has news of my arrival been printed in the local paper? Everyone seems to know who I am."

"Well, it's not hard to tell, dear. You do have that accent. And believe me, the arrival of a pretty, unattached lass on this island doesn't go unnoticed. Have you had any marriage proposals yet? Because if you're interested in staying, I'm sure I could find you some. I'm the local matchmaker as well as the librarian."

"You're joking, right?"

"The population on Trall has been falling for thirty years now. We don't joke about things like that. But then, you may not be impressed with our bachelors, especially after setting your eyes on that lovely man, Will Donovan. He's enough to turn a girl's head clear 'round, isn't he?"

Claire's cheeks heated. She needed to change the subject. "I—I was looking for an old guidebook for the island."

"We have some new guidebooks on the table near the door," Beatrice said. "They're just three euros twenty."

Claire had paged through the island's guidebook last night at the inn, while she was waiting for Will to come home, and there'd been no mention of the spring. "I'm actually wondering about the legend of the Druid spring. My grandmother told me about it. She visited the island almost fifty years ago and got water from the spring. I thought I'd take a bottle of the water back home to her."

"Ah. That's what brings most of the tourists to the island. When people think of Trall, they think of the spring."

"I was hoping I'd be able to find it. But no one wants to tell me where it is."

"And does it surprise you, that? Those who hate the tourists trampling over our lovely island would prefer the legend be forgotten. And those who depend on the legend for business want to maintain its mystique. If everyone knew where it was, then they'd simply visit, fill up their canteens and off they'd go. It's the search that keeps them here."

"So you're not going to tell me?" Claire said.

"Of course not. But our library does have a nice collection of old guidebooks. Right over there next to the travel books." Beatrice gave her a wink. "And now, I think I'll be havin' my tea. Can I bring you a cup?"

"Yes," Claire replied with a smile. "That would be nice."

After an hour of paging through the guidebooks, two cups of tea and a plate of shortbread cookies, Claire had her answer—or at least what she thought was a list of clues. She tucked the hastily scribbled map into her pocket and walked back to the Range Rover. She had a bottle of water in the car that she could empty and fill with water from the spring. And after that, her mission on Trall would be complete.

Claire sat inside the truck, her hands clutching the wheel. She'd have what she came for and she could go home. But she didn't want to go home, not yet. The thought of heading back to Chicago left her with a strange and empty feeling.

She groaned softly, then leaned forward and rested her head on the steering wheel. Images of Will Donovan swam in her head and she tried to push them away. Something had happened between them last night, some strange, magical connection. Something crazy and exciting and Claire wasn't ready to leave that behind.

A tiny sigh slipped from her lips. Had she really ever loved Eric at all? She'd certainly forgotten him quickly enough. For the present, all she could think about was the handsome innkeeper who had seduced her last night, made her moan with ecstasy. And if she found this water, then she'd no longer have an excuse to stay and enjoy the pleasures he offered.

A knock sounded on the window and, startled, Claire sat up. A young man waved at her with a toothy smile. Claire flipped the ignition and then pressed the button for the power window. "Hello," she said.

"Are you the American?" he asked.

"Yes."

"Would you care to have supper with me tonight?"

"I—I don't know you," Claire said.

He blushed, then wiped his hand on his trousers before sticking it inside the window. "Derrick. I'm Derrick Dooly. I run the petrol station on the island. You need your car fixed, I'm the man for the job. I make a good livin'. And I'd be faithful, that I would."

Claire's eyes went wide. "I—I appreciate the invitation, Derrick," she said. "But I'm really not…well, I'm not sure…" She drew a deep breath. "The truth is, I'm probably going to be leaving in a few days and I wouldn't want to…to break your heart."

He considered her answer, then shook his head. "Oh, ye wouldn't break my heart. I'm a tough one, I am."

"I see. Well, perhaps I could have dinner with you, under one condition. Do you know where the Druid spring is?"

"Oh, sure. Most folks on the island know. Or they say they do."

"Could you show me?"

Derrick scowled. "Well, now…" He removed his

cap and scratched his head. "I'm not sure I could do that, miss. It's a closely guarded secret, you see. And I wouldn't want to be the one bloke who lets the cat out of the bag, so to speak."

"And I don't have supper plans for the evening," she said, sighing dramatically.

"Well," Derrick said, "I suppose it wouldn't hurt. As long as you promise not to tell anyone that I told ye."

Claire smiled. "Hop in," she said. Dinner with Derrick Dooly was a small price to pay for finding the spring. She'd make it an early date, nibble at her food and be back at the inn in time to eat with Will. She wasn't leaving Trall without that water.

4

HE'D BEEN WAITING for nearly three hours for Claire to return to the inn. When she wasn't back by sunset, Will had rung the pub and learned that she'd come in an hour before and was enjoying a drink with Sorcha, Derrick Dooly and a few of the other bachelors from the island.

He'd decided to sit tight, but as the evening wore on, Will became concerned about her driving the narrow lanes back to the inn. Though there wasn't a constabulary on the island to arrest her for driving while drunk, he didn't want his truck run up against a wall or, worse yet, Claire injured.

Will grabbed his keys from the reception desk and headed out the back of the house to the Mercedes sedan parked in the carriage house. The car was one of the few things he'd kept from his previous life—the car, the bed and the house outside of Killarney.

There'd been a time when he'd considered himself the luckiest of men. An interest in computers had led to a passion for software development. When he'd invented a new type of facial recognition software and formed a company to market it, he'd instantly become a millionaire. Over the next three years, he'd been hailed as Ireland's computer wunderkind. Everything he'd touched turned to gold. People began to call him the Bill Gates of Ireland, a reference he'd come to loathe.

And then, a computer giant had come calling and offered to buy his company. When the money became to good to refuse, he grabbed it. Will had thought to turn around and start another company, this one bigger and better. But after a few months without the crushing responsibility of running a business, he began to realize that he didn't want to return to that life. A few months turned to a year and then another. And four years later, he was living on this sleepy little island, running his family's inn and occasionally accepting consulting contracts.

He had plenty of money to live on, but he'd placed his life on hold, waiting for something interesting to come along, something that he might once again feel passionate about. And now, for the first time in years, he felt…something. Will just wasn't sure what it was.

He found the Range Rover parked near the pub. When he walked inside the Jolly Farmer, he peered through the smoke to see Claire, surrounded by a rowdy group of men, tossing darts at the dartboard. Sorcha was nearby, taking bets and cheering Claire on. Will watched for a while, then wove through the boisterous crowd to stand beside Sorcha.

"You got her drunk?"

Sorcha glanced up. "Ah, William! So you've decided to come and compete for Claire's favor. Derrick is determined to give you a run for your money, aren't you, Derrick! And don't be silly. I didn't get her drunk. She did that entirely on her own."

"I'm going to take her back to the inn now."

Sorcha shrugged. "That would probably be best. One more chocolate martini and she'll be completely bolloxed. You'll have to carry her out of here."

Will stepped up to Claire and took her hand. "Time to go," he said.

"Already?" Claire asked. The crowd of men groaned in disappointment as Will tossed a ten-euro note on the table.

Claire turned to Derrick and threw her arms around his neck, giving him a fierce hug. "Thank you for the lovely dinner," she said. "And don't worry. You'll find a nice girl to marry. I know you will."

Will took her hand and led her to the door. Claire turned around and gave her new friends a wave and they all cheered before she stepped outside. He helped her into the Mercedes, then slipped in behind the wheel.

"They were all so nice," Claire said. "Why can't all men be as nice as they are? I had three marriage proposals. And Beatrice Fraser said she could get me more." She sighed dramatically. "I'd really love to be married someday."

Will frowned as he pulled the car out onto the street. The liquor had obviously loosened her tongue. He sent her a sideways glance. And her emotions, he mused. By the light from the dashboard he saw tears swimming in her eyes.

"Are you crying?"

"No," she murmured.

A tear dribbled down her cheek, so he pulled the car over to the side of the road and stopped.

"What's wrong? Did Sorcha say something to hurt you?"

"She told me I deserved better," Claire said, wiping the tears away with her jacket sleeve.

"Better than me?"

"No," she said, shaking her head. "Better than him."

"Who?"

"Eric. My fiancé."

Will's breath froze in his throat. "You're engaged?"

"Yes. I mean no. I thought I was. But—" An odd look came over her face. "Oh, God. I don't feel so well." She opened the door of the Mercedes and stumbled out. Will watched as she bent over at the side of the road and threw up. It had been a long time since he'd been that drunk and he wondered how much of their conversation she'd remember in the morning.

She leaned back against the front fender of the sedan, drawing deeply of the chilly night air, then crawled back inside.

"Better?" he asked.

"Much," she murmured.

Will threw the car back into gear and pulled out onto the road. They drove the rest of the way to the inn in silence, Will mulling over what he'd just learned about Claire's life in Chicago. What kind of chancer would have let a woman like her get away? A guy would have to be a bleedin' eedjit. She was beautiful and sexy and sweet and smart. Women like Claire O'Connor didn't come along every day.

When they reached the inn, Will parked the car in the front drive and helped Claire inside. She stumbled up the stairs and the moment she got to her room, she began to tear off her clothes. "I don't know why I even bothered to come here," she said. "Why do I want this man back? He obviously never loved me."

She pulled her jumper over her head and then got tangled in it. Will stepped up and helped her remove it, then tossed it aside. She was unsteady on her feet and he grabbed her waist as she pulled off her T-shirt. "Do you still love him?" he asked.

She crinkled up her nose and considered his question for a long moment, then looked up at him with a blank expression. "Have you ever been in love?"

"No," Will said. He'd thought he was, once, but in the end, after she'd left him, he'd realized that what he'd felt wasn't love at all.

"Consider yourself lucky," Claire muttered, wagging her finger at him. She reached down and unhooked the front clasp of her bra, then let it fall to the floor, before starting on the button of her jeans.

Will couldn't help but take in the sight of her, half-naked. She didn't seem to be aware of what she was doing. He swallowed hard. Unfortunately, he was painfully aware of what she was doing to *him.*

"It's just that we were so perfect for each other. We both wanted the same things. We shared the same interests. We had a future planned and then, in one day, it was over. Poof!" She threw her arms out dramatically and wavered on her feet, nearly tipping backward before he caught her.

"So you want this guy back?"

"Of course," she said, walking into the bathroom. "I think." She frowned slightly. "Wouldn't you?"

He watched as she brushed her teeth, finding it fascinating to see her engage in such a mundane task. She made even dental hygiene seem sexy. Especially when performed topless.

Claire wiped her mouth on a towel then walked back into the room. "That's why I came here."

Realization slowly dawned. "For the water," he murmured.

"My grandmother told me all about it. How I could use it to get him back. And I found the spring today. Derrick Dooly showed me where it was." She clapped her hand to her mouth. "Oops. I wasn't supposed to say that. It's a secret."

Will was tempted to tell her the truth. That the Druid spring was nothing more than a hoax invented by his great-grandfather to get more tourists to visit the island. Over the years, the truth of the spring had been forgotten, replaced by the myth and Sorcha's self-promotion. "Really," he said.

"I have a bottle of the water." She glanced around the room. "In the truck. I left it in the truck."

"And how did you end up at the pub?"

"I saw Sorcha in town after I had supper with Derrick and she invited us for a drink at the pub. She bought me a Guinness and I bought her a chocolate martini. And then we had another and another. We just drank chocolate martinis all night long."

"And you're drunk."

"I'm not drunk," Claire said, unzipping her jeans. She slid them over her hips and stepped out of them. Then she glanced up at Will and wrapped her arms around his neck. "Are we going to stand here all night chatting or are you going to take me to bed?"

Will groaned inwardly. Didn't this make a fine show? All he'd been thinking about was the next time they'd crawl into bed together and now she was offering herself up. The only problem was that she wouldn't remember much of what had happened the next morning. So, to satisfy her wishes or to be a gentleman…again? Will knew the answer before he asked the question, but that didn't make it any easier to refuse.

"Why don't you crawl under the covers," he said, taking her hand and pulling her toward the bed. "I'm going to go down and get you something to settle your stomach."

She did as she was told, but then pulled him down on top of her. His gaze fell to her mouth and Will couldn't fight the urge to kiss her, just once.

Her lips parted and he took a taste—sweet, like cinnamon from her toothpaste. Her tongue teased at his, inviting him to explore further and he accepted.

They kissed for a long time, doing nothing more than learning precisely how their mouths fit together—and how pleasurable it was. Hell, he could spend a day or two kissing her and never tire of the experience. There was so much he didn't know about her and Will wanted to learn it all, slowly and carefully.

Her hand moved down to the front of his jeans and she rubbed him through the faded denim. He was already hard and the friction was enough to make him want to tear off his clothes and lose himself inside of her. Was he willing to gamble that they'd have at least one more night together? Or would she wake tomorrow morning, pack her bags and take her little bottle of magic water back to Chicago and to the man she really wanted?

No man should have to be faced with this choice, Will mused as he kissed her neck. Damn Sorcha Mulroony and her meddling. If she hadn't invited Claire to the pub, then there wouldn't have been a choice at all. They'd have spent the night in bed, engaged in passionate, earth-shattering sex. He pushed up on his elbow and smoothed the hair out of her eyes.

"I'm going to get you a cup of tea," he said.

"I don't want tea," Claire protested.

"With a bit of milk and some sugar, it will calm your stomach. You'll thank me for it in the morning."

"You promise you'll come back? Because that's not all I want to thank you for in the morning." She grinned. "If you know what I mean."

Will chuckled. "Yes, I know what you mean. I'll be right back." He rolled off the bed and reached down to tuck the covers in around her. "Close your eyes and rest."

She moaned softly, then buried her face in the down pillow. He stood over her for a few minutes, watching as her breathing grew more regular. He grabbed the glass from the bedside table and filled it from the tap in the bathroom, then set it back in place. And when he was sure she was sleeping soundly, Will bent over and kissed her forehead.

He wasn't sure what she'd remember in the morning, but he would be damn sure that when they finally did have sex—if they did—it would be burned indelibly in her mind. Will turned off the light and walked out of the room, closing the door behind him.

But when he got downstairs, instead of heading back to his own bed, he grabbed his keys and slipped out the front door. The Mercedes was where he'd left it. He hopped inside, started the car and headed back into the village.

He parked in front of the Range Rover and got out. The doors were locked and Will searched for the spare key on his key ring. Claire was unaware that there was virtually no crime on the island. He never locked his car and only locked the inn to keep Dickie O'Malley out of his scotch.

Will found the bottle of water on the passenger side seat. He grabbed it, unscrewed the cap and prepared to dump it. If Claire were forced to go back to the spring tomorrow, then she wouldn't be able to leave, giving him at least one more night with her.

But before he could turn the bottle upside down, Will decided that the water might be put to better use. He'd never believed in any of the island's Druid magic, but it couldn't hurt to give it a try. Tomorrow morning, he'd make Claire a nice pot of tea or a jug of juice. And he'd sit and watch her drink it down. And then he'd have a drink himself. And if there were anything at all to the magic of the water, he'd be the first one to know it.

CLAIRE STARED at her bloodshot eyes in the bathroom mirror. Since she'd come to Ireland, she hadn't been herself. She barely recognized the woman staring back at her. She'd traveled across an ocean to find a magic spring. Then she'd messed around with the very first man she'd met on Trall. Actually, the third man, behind Captain Billy and the farmer with the horse. Then, she'd gotten herself stumbling drunk not once but twice, something she'd never done in her entire life. And finally, she'd managed to forget the previous evening. Not entirely, but most of the details were pretty hazy.

She did remember throwing up on the side of the road and coming up to her room with Will and attempting to seduce him. And there was a niggling memory of mentioning her fiancé, though she couldn't be sure if she'd actually said Eric's name out loud or if she'd just been thinking it. Either way, she didn't relish facing Will over breakfast—or lunch, if she chose to hide out in her room a bit longer.

Claire grabbed some clean clothes and got dressed, then slowly made her way downstairs to the kitchen. Will was there, standing at the worktable, a newspaper spread out in front of him. He wore a faded T-shirt and jeans that hung low on his waist. As always, his hair looked mussed, but he had shaved and Claire was surprised at how young he looked without the scruffy beard.

She stepped into the kitchen and pasted a tight smile on her face. "Morning."

He glanced up and sent her a grin in return. "You don't look any worse for your night at the pub," he said. "How do you feel?"

"I'm not sure yet," Claire said, reaching out to brace her hand on the edge of the worktable. "How do you think I should feel?"

He raised his eyebrow. "Tired?"

"How about embarrassed?" Claire offered.

"Are you asking if you did anything to embarrass yourself?" He seemed amused by the question and Claire groaned inwardly.

"Did I? As I remember, I didn't do anything too humiliating but things are kind of fuzzy."

"Nothing too humiliating," Will reassured her. "Except for throwing up on the side of the road. And that striptease you did for the boys at the pub. But I really wouldn't call that humiliating as they seemed to enjoy it."

Claire gasped and Will held up his hand. "Just joking," he said. "Not about the throwing up, but the striptease. I must have just imagined that."

"Chocolate martinis," she said, shaking her head. "Not the best choice, especially on top of that pint of Guinness."

Will stared down at his newspaper. "And then, of course, you tried to seduce me."

Claire's eyes went wide. Her memory was correct on that point. "Did I succeed?"

"No. I thought it best we save that until you were sober. But I have a few free hours this afternoon," he teased. "You're welcome to try again."

Claire's cheeks warmed with embarrassment. "I'll let you know if I'm up to it." She reached up and rubbed her temples. "Do you have an aspirin? My head is throbbing."

"I have something better," he said. "I figured you might feel a touch green this morning and I made a special Trall remedy. Its formulation is highly secret, but it's guaranteed to get rid of the hangover." He opened the refrigerator and bent over, searching the shelves.

Claire couldn't help but admire the view he presented, a tight backside covered in faded denim. He obviously didn't spend hours in the gym, but Will's body was just about as perfect as it could get. He was tall and lean, with an impossibly narrow waist. His shoulders were broad and his arms finely muscled. He moved with an easy grace and she imagined that he was probably a good dancer.

Picturing him naked was remedy enough, she mused. Enough to get her blood pumping and her pulse racing. He turned back to her with a small pitcher in his hand. He set the pitcher on the worktable, then grabbed a glass and filled it with ice. "Now, you have to drink this right down, straightaway, for it to work."

Claire picked up the glass and sniffed at it. "Tomato juice? And beer? If there's vodka in it, then you've made a Bloody Mary. Do you want me to get drunk all over again?"

"We Irish are firm believers in hair of the dog," he said. "Besides, there are some other secret ingredients in it that will make you feel better."

He poured himself a glass and knocked it against hers before taking a long swallow. Reluctantly, she picked up her glass and, as instructed, gulped it down. For a brief moment, Claire was afraid it would all come right back up again. But then, a few moments later, an odd sensation came over her. Her stomach stopped churning and her head stopped aching. She felt a pleasant warmth course through her limbs.

"Better?" Will asked.

"Yes," she said, amazed. "Wow, that worked really fast. I actually feel pretty good."

Will set a plate stacked with raisin scones in front of her. "Do you have plans for the day?"

Claire shook her head. "I thought I'd just crawl back into bed for a while." She took a bite of a scone. "I mean, because I need the sleep. But now, I'm not sure." She paused. "I'd like to go to Sorcha's celebration tonight. And maybe go over to the mainland and take a drive around before I go home."

His gaze met hers for a brief moment, then Will looked away. "I promised Sorcha I'd help her haul some of her things out to the stone circle for the celebration tonight. And I've got guests arriving on the one o'clock ferry. But we could go tomorrow…or the next day."

Claire nibbled on the pastry. "What does she do out there?"

"There's music and dancing and incantations. And then she sacrifices a virgin," Will said as he refolded the paper.

"A virgin? I thought you were joking about that."

"You don't have to worry. You're safe," he said. "Aren't you?"

He enjoyed teasing her. And in truth, she thought it was fun, too. Eric had always been so serious. The man had no sense of humor. Oddly, that hadn't been a quality she'd put on her list, but in hindsight, she realized how important it was. "I'm not so sure. While I was taking in the sights yesterday, I think I must have met every unmarried man on the island, including a few who were old enough to be my grandfather. How is it that everyone knows about me?"

"If Sorcha knew sorcery as well as she knows gossip, we'd all be toads and she'd be the Queen of England,"

Will said. "Hell, you're an interesting topic. You're single and pretty and nearly every tourist who visits Trall comes for the Druid spring. It's like a romantic quest, so they arrive as couples. We don't get unattached women on Trall. And when we do, they usually don't choose to spend the rest of their lives stuck on an island off the coast of Ireland." He met her gaze. "We find you intriguing. *I* find you intriguing."

"You do?"

Will stepped over to her, pressing her back against the edge of the worktable as his hands spanned her waist. "Are you feeling better now?"

Claire nodded, her eyes skimming the handsome features of his face. He pressed a kiss to her temple and she sighed softly, enjoying the warmth of his lips on her skin.

"A guy could get used to having this for breakfast," he said.

Claire drew back and then gently touched her lips to his. "You choose," she teased. "Me or a raisin scone."

"You," he said without hesitation.

"Me or a raisin scone right out of the oven."

This time he thought about it for a long moment, his brow furrowed into a frown. "Oh, tough choice, that. Right out of the oven?"

Claire playfully slapped his shoulder. How was it that she felt so comfortable with this man after only knowing him a few days? Was it because there were no expectations between them? No future for her to worry over? Everything with Will was so simple that there was no need to be serious.

"If that's your decision," she said, "then I'll leave you to your scones."

Will's grip tightened around her waist as she tried to walk away. He picked her up and set her on the worktable, then stepped between her legs and slowly began to undo the buttons on her cardigan. "I can't decide without a taste," he said. He pressed his lips to the base of her neck, then moved lower and lower as he unbuttoned her blouse, dropping a kiss in each spot until he'd reached her bra.

He quickly dispatched the clasp in front and continued his journey to the last button of her blouse. When it was undone, he smoothed his hands beneath the crisp cotton fabric, pulling her into his body. "You," he said. "I'd rather have you than a warm scone. Any day and twice on Sundays."

"Good to know," Claire replied. "Is there any food that you'd prefer instead of me?"

"Right now, I can't think of another taste that would satisfy me."

"What about George and Glynis?"

Will shook his head. "No, I don't want to taste them."

"They might walk in."

"They've had their breakfast and are off taking a hike around the island."

Claire slid back onto the table, then slowly leaned back, bracing her arms behind her. "Well then, taste away," she murmured.

With a low chuckle, Will crawled up on the table, sliding along her body until their hips were pressed together. The contact between them was electric and

Claire forgot all about her queasy stomach and her nagging headache. Though Will's hangover remedy might have done the job, this encounter would certainly put the color back into her cheeks.

Will pressed her back onto the table, his hands on either side of her head, then bent to kiss her. But he seemed more intent on teasing her and drawing his tongue along her lower lip, then pulling back. Every effort to capture his mouth in a lazy kiss was thwarted until Claire slipped her hand through his hair and pulled him down on top of her.

He growled as he kissed her. The connection between them was powerful, so instant and intense that it took Claire's breath away. She wanted to cast aside their clothes, to indulge in every single sexual fantasy she'd ever had. Touching his body seemed to be the only thing she could focus on and her fingers tugged frantically at his clothes.

The fact that they were doing this in the middle of the kitchen made it even more dangerous and Claire found that the danger wasn't a fear but a turn-on. Why did her characteristic restraint seem to disappear the moment Will Donovan touched her? Was it him or had she simply become a different person the moment she'd landed in Ireland?

Her hands slid beneath his T-shirt to smooth over the hard muscles of his back. But it wasn't enough for Will and he got to his knees and pulled the shirt off over his head.

The kissing and touching was slow and easy at first, playful, as if they were both testing each other's responses. Clothing was brushed aside to make way for a gentle exploration. She'd touched him before, had lost herself in the beauty of his body, and wondered what it might be like to completely surrender to their desire.

A sudden surge of doubt welled up inside of her. Was she really ready for this? It might change everything. She might want him for more than just a night or two. Claire cast aside the first practical thought she'd had since arriving in Ireland. She wanted Will and what happened afterward didn't matter.

"I have to say," he mused, "when I bought this table, I didn't imagine using it in this way. But I did imagine this." He ran his palm from her collarbone to her belly.

"You imagined this?" Claire asked.

"From the moment you walked in the door all wet and miserable."

"Show me how you imagined it," she said.

He rolled to her side and braced his head on his hand, his fingers skimming over her breasts in a tantalizing tease. He kissed her again, then crawled off the table and held out his hand. "Come with me."

"Where are we going?"

"Someplace a lot more comfortable than this table." Will grabbed her waist as she slid to the edge, stepping between her legs to kiss her again. Smoothing his hands along her thighs, he wrapped her legs around his waist and picked her up.

They walked toward a small door at the far side of the kitchen, where a small sign on the door spelled out Private. Will kicked it open to reveal a comfortable sitting room filled with overstuffed furniture, expensive stereo equipment and books. "I wondered where you lived," she said, glancing around.

He walked through the room and into another, this one dominated by a massive four-poster bed. "This is what I imagined," he said. "You. In my bed."

Claire nuzzled her face into Will's neck. This was him, the man he was, in the place he lived. In her mind, he hadn't had a life before she'd come into it. But he spent his nights here, alone in this huge bed with the rumpled linens and the rich fabric hangings. "It looks medieval," she said.

"Elizabethan," he said. "I bought it back when I had money to waste on important antiques and I had a huge house to furnish. I've gotten rid of almost everything else except this. I just couldn't part with it."

The bed was higher than the worktable and when he set her on the edge of the mattress her legs hugged his torso. Claire wrapped her arms around his neck as he kissed her breasts, his tongue lingering over each nipple.

Though her pulse raced, Claire felt a sense of languor envelop her, as if she and Will were alone on an island, this island of a bed, with nothing but time between them. The real world would intrude on them once the guests arrived. But for now, she still had Will all to herself.

He brushed her shirt from her shoulders along with her bra, then moved to her jeans, tugging them off until only her panties were left. Claire closed her eyes and let the sensation of his hands on her skin fill her thoughts.

He seemed to be fascinated by her body, eager to learn every inch of skin, every soft curve. His lips trailed after his hands and when he reached her belly, Will pushed her back on the bed and hooked his fingers through the waistband of her panties. He drew them down along her legs, but he didn't seem to be in a hurry to discard the rest of his clothes. The button on his jeans was open, the zipper was down and she could see his erection pushing at the faded fabric.

His lips kissed a path along her inner thigh and Claire held her breath. His lips were warm on her skin and his tongue left a tantalizing imprint. When he gently drew her legs up, Claire knew what he wanted. Yet she wasn't prepared for the shock of his mouth on her sex.

A gasp burst from her lips as he began to taste her with his tongue. For a moment, she couldn't inhale, the force of her reaction stealing the breath from her lungs. Wild currents of pleasure raced through her body and she reached down to run her fingers through his hair.

He knew exactly what he was doing, exactly how to tease for maximum effect. Claire tried to maintain her grip on reality, but before long, she found herself lost in a fog of desire and sensation. She longed to have him deep inside of her, to feel him move above her, but she had lost any control she might have had over the situation.

He controlled her pulse and her breathing, the tiny moans that slipped involuntarily from her lips, her shivers and shudders. Claire had never felt anything quite so intense as this slow seduction. Every time she approached the edge, he drew her back.

And then he brought her up again, the need surging inside of her. Claire murmured his name, a soft plea to bring her to completion. This time, Will didn't stop. When she reached the edge, he carried her over. Claire's composure shattered as the orgasm rocked her body. Spasm after spasm coursed through her body, waves of pleasure overwhelming her.

When it was over, he crawled up on the bed and gathered her into his arms, pulling her body into the curve of his. Claire closed her eyes, completely sated, drowsy with satisfaction. He'd touched her so intimately, yet she felt no inhibition, no regret. It seemed right that Will should possess her body in that way.

Had she held the same power over him, the means to make him ache for release at her touch? They'd taken one more step toward an act that seemed almost inevitable now. Claire knew she couldn't allow herself to fall in love with him, and making love to him might just signal the end of her resolve.

Could she trust herself to surrender her body, yet control her heart? Could she trust him? What did he want from her? Claire sighed softly and she felt his embrace tighten around her waist. It was so easy to forget Eric when she was with Will, to imagine that there might be someone else who could inhabit her future.

Maybe it was time to head home, before leaving became impossible. Claire wove her fingers through his and pressed her lips to the back of his hand. Tomorrow. She'd think about leaving tomorrow. Tonight, she would give herself to him, completely and utterly.

WILL GLANCED at the clock on the bedside table. It was nearly noon and guests would begin arriving in just over an hour. If he crawled out of bed now, he'd have just enough time to help Sorcha before he needed to get back to check in the new arrivals.

He drew a deep breath and closed his eyes. When he'd laced Claire's hangover remedy with Druid water, he hadn't expected it to work. It had been a silly experiment. But after what had happened between them, Will was forced to consider that maybe there was something to Sorcha's magic.

He cursed inwardly. No, there wasn't! From the moment Claire had arrived, there'd been a tension between them that could only be eased by full-on seduction. It wasn't magic, it was lust, pure and simple. And though they'd taken one more step toward their ultimate pleasure, Will wasn't sure they ought to take another.

He wanted nothing more than to make love to her, to lose himself inside of her. But he couldn't wish the real world away, as much as he might like to do so. For the past few days, he'd been living out a fantasy, fascinated by a beautiful, seductive woman. But sooner or later, she'd go home and he'd be left with just memories of the desire they shared.

It was so easy to want her. When she looked at him, she didn't see anything but a man she desired. She didn't see the money, the power, the possibility of a comfortable life spent draining his bank accounts. She saw the man he was, plainly and simply. With Claire, he didn't have to question her motives and that made it easier to want her.

He gently brushed a strand of hair from her temple, then pressed his lips to her forehead. She stirred and opened her eyes. "I have to go," he murmured. "If I don't leave now, Sorcha will kick my arse around the island. And I won't be back in time for my guests."

Claire nodded, then crawled out of bed with him. She was naked and Will took the opportunity to enjoy the sight, until she found a denim shirt of his and slipped it on. "I could help you," she said, wrapping the shirt around her body and sitting on the edge of the bed. "I mean, I could help Sorcha. How much longer would that give us?"

Will smiled. "A half hour, maybe forty-five minutes, tops."

"We can do a lot in forty-five minutes," she said.

Will groaned softly as he pulled her back into bed, aroused by the prospect of a few more minutes kissing and touching. But as Claire ran her fingers from his chest to his belly, he suspected that a few minutes weren't going to be enough.

Her hand slipped beneath the waistband of his jeans and he chuckled softly, acutely aware of his reaction to her touch. "What are you doing?" he asked.

"Do I have to explain?" she teased. "After what you did to me, I assumed you had some experience with women."

"I've never been with a woman quite like you," he said.

"American?"

Will shook his head.

"Blonde?"

"No, that isn't it." She wrapped her fingers around his shaft and Will sucked in a sharp breath. "I—I mean, that's it, right there. But that's not what I was talking about. I've never been with a woman who can—" He held his breath as she began to stroke him. "Who can make me feel the way you do."

Claire slid down along his body and when she reached his waist, she pulled back his jeans and dropped a kiss on the skin near his hip, then she bit, just hard enough to leave a mark.

Will stretched his arms over his head, grabbing onto the bed as she continued to tease him. He was ready to get as good as he gave and when she finally took him between her lips, he had to close his eyes and count backward from five thousand to control his need for release.

In the past, Will had always enjoyed this particular part of foreplay. There were times when he found it more pleasurable then sex. But for some reason, this wasn't about him. This was about Claire, about her ability to offer herself to him, to focus on his needs without a care for her own. She was determined to please him and he wanted nothing more to give her that.

Though he knew there had been other men in her life, even a fiancé, he could still believe that what they shared was new to both of them. They fit together so perfectly that their experiences with each other seemed magnified in intensity.

She tugged at his jeans, trying to pull them down over his hips, and when she couldn't, Will helped her. But doing so only made his control waver. Her fingers and her lips now caressed the length of his shaft, drawing him in and out of her warm mouth. He felt a knot slowly tighten in his belly and Will knew he was close. She felt it, too, because slowly, Claire increased her pace.

And then, just as he was about to give himself over, she stopped.

Will opened his eyes and looked down at her.

"Did you hear that?" she asked.

"Hear what?"

"Someone is out there. I think George and Glynis are back."

"Oh, bloody hell," Will muttered. "Maybe if we stay real quiet, they'll go away." They waited, but when Will heard his name called, he cursed. "I guess not."

Claire smiled as she crawled off the bed. "We can always pick this up later."

"That's easy for you to say." He stared down at his raging erection, knowing that it would take more than a few minutes to go away. "I'll get an apron or something in the kitchen. You stay here."

He quickly stuffed himself back into his jeans, then grabbed a T-shirt from the pile of clean laundry in his closet. Claire seemed to take great amusement in his situation and before he left, he kissed her thoroughly, plundering her mouth with his tongue until he'd left her breathless.

"We will pick this up later," he warned.

As he stepped to the door, she hurled a pillow at him. Will hurried through the kitchen, grabbing a towel on his way through and tucking it into the front of his jeans. He found the elderly couple waiting in the front hall.

"Sorry," he called. "I didn't hear you come in. What can I do for you?"

"We were hoping to borrow a small bucket and a spade," George said.

"We've come across a lovely little beach with sea glass. I have a friend who makes it into jewelry," Glynis added.

"Yes," Will said. "Well, you're welcome to look in the carriage house. I'm sure you'll find what you need in there."

"Right-o," George said. "We'll do that."

Will watched them walk out, then hurried back to the kitchen. He grabbed his T-shirt and stepped back through the door to his rooms.

He found her sitting on the center of the bed, staring at a framed photo. "Pretty girl," she said, holding it up.

"My sister," Will explained. "Maureen. That was taken before she got married. She has three kids now."

"Just one sister?" Claire asked.

He nodded. "How about you?"

"No sisters, although I always wanted one. I have five older brothers."

"Five?"

Claire nodded. "Patrick, Michael, David, John and James. I used to imagine that they had somehow stolen me from my real parents, just as a joke, and then never bothered to give me back. I'd dream that my real parents would find me and take me away to a beautiful apartment, overlooking the Lincoln Park Zoo." She handed him the photo. "Any pictures of other special people?"

"Wait," he said. He walked out to the parlor and retrieved his digital camera from his desk. When he stepped back into the bedroom, he snapped a photo of Claire, just before she put her hands over her face and screamed. "There," he said with a grin.

"I'm not your girlfriend or anything, Will Donovan."

"Oh, you want pictures of all my old lovers? Well then, I have albums. Boxes. Cartons." In truth, he hadn't kept any mementos from previous relationships. There didn't seem to be a point since they'd all ended. But now he had a photo of Claire, something to keep after she left Ireland.

She grabbed her bra and put it on, then slipped into her shirt and pale blue sweater. Her panties were on the floor beside the bed and Will picked them up and held them out to her, dangling them from one finger. She grabbed them. "What am I supposed to do for Sorcha?" she asked.

"Come back to bed," Will demanded. "George and Glynis are gone and we have fifteen minutes to finish what you started."

"No, that can wait. Tell me."

He groaned. "There are some boxes stacked out in the carriage house. They're heavy, so I'll help you load them. Just take them out to the stone circle. She has some guys out there who will be able to unload them."

Claire grabbed his hand. "Come on then, let's go."

He tugged her back into bed, pulling her up until she straddled his hips. His hands circled her waist and his gaze skimmed her body. "Tell me something," he began. The question had been plaguing his mind and he knew he oughtn't ask. But he wanted to know where he stood, how much longer he had. Just so he could put this all in perspective. "Last night, you mentioned you had a fiancé. Is that true?"

Claire held her breath, as if the word *fiancé* had caused her some sort of pain. "Had," she said. "Past tense. He dumped me. Actually, he wasn't officially my fiancé, but I'm sure he was about to ask me to marry him. And he'd bought a ring, or at least I think he had. I had it all planned out and then..." She drew a ragged breath. "Maybe he was just a guy I lived with."

"Past tense," Will repeated. Her answer was unexpected. And it brought a small amount of relief. "There's something else I need to know."

"The answer is, I don't know," Claire said.

"You didn't hear the question."

"I know what it is. You were going to ask if I still loved him. And my answer is, I don't know."

"I was going to ask how long you were planning to stay," Will countered.

"Oh," she said. Her cheeks grew pink with a blush. "My ticket says I'm supposed to go back today. But I guess that's not going to happen."

Will shook his head. "Stay through the weekend."

His request seemed to take a few moments to register. "I—I don't know."

"I won't charge you for the room, as long as you sleep in here," he said with a smile. "Hell, I won't charge you if we sleep in your bed. And if there's a fee to change your ticket, I'll take care of that."

"I'm out of a job, Will. I'm going to need to get back and look for work. And my apartment is going condo, so I'm going to have to look for a new place to live and—"

"I'm not asking you to stay forever," he said. "Just a few more days. Extend your vacation. What's the harm?"

"All right," Claire said reluctantly. "But I'll pay for my own room."

"Only if you sleep alone," he replied.

"And who says I'm going to sleep with you?" she said, raising her eyebrow and fixing him with a haughty look.

"You never know what might happen," he replied. Hell, he had three more days. From where he sat, that was close to a lifetime. And the truth was, neither one of them knew what would happen. And that made it all the more exciting to anticipate.

5

BONFIRES BURNED along the perimeter of the stone circle, and sparks swirled up into the night sky, carried by a damp wind. Claire had never seen or heard anything like it, the incessant beat of drums and the eerie sound of tin whistles, the whirl of white robes and unbound hair as Sorcha and her friends danced around the stone altar.

She and Will had arrived after the ceremony had started and a large crowd had already gathered on the hillside above the circle. Will had informed her that almost everyone from the island put in an appearance, or risked Sorcha's wrath. A basket was passed after the first ceremony and was filled with coins and bills. Claire marveled at Sorcha's ability to make a living with her magic, only to learn that the money made at Samhain went to buy books for the village library.

"This is amazing," Claire said, sitting cross-legged on the blanket Will had laid out. "It's like a mix of Halloween and a Super Bowl halftime show."

"It's the closest thing we have to spectacle on Trall," he said. "On the mainland they have their football matches and rock concerts. Here were have Sorcha and her Druid priestesses."

The women spun around the fires, tossing something into the flames from reed baskets. "What are they doing?"

"Samhain is traditionally the end of the old year and the beginning of the new. They're thanking the gods for a plentiful harvest season. And Sorcha also honors those who have gone on to the spirit world during the year."

"It's very…stirring," Claire said. "The drums and shouting."

Will nodded. "This is pretty tame compared to Beltane. Sorcha and her friends are known to throw off their robes and dance naked around the fire when the weather is a bit warmer. Needless to say, the tourist crowd is much bigger for that celebration."

"That would be interesting to see," Claire commented.

"You should go down there and dance," he suggested, nodding in the direction of the stone circle.

Claire gasped. She never was one for dancing, not even in nightclubs. "Me?"

"Lots of the women do. It's part of the fun. Sorcha says it's supposed to give women power over men."

"I couldn't," Claire said, shaking her head.

"If you want to experience everything Trall has to offer, this would be part of it."

Claire gave him a sideways glance, then giggled. He was challenging her and though she was usually a bit timid in front of people, she wanted to accept this challenge. "You don't think I will, do you?"

"No," Will said.

"What will you give me if I do?"

"Name your price," Will teased.

"I don't know what to ask for."

He smiled. "You want power over men? I'll agree to be your slave for an entire day—and night."

"What does that mean? You'll do my laundry, make my bed, rub my bunions?"

"I'll do whatever you want me to do," Will said with a devilish grin.

Claire thought about it for a moment. The offer really was too good to resist. And having Will under her complete control for twenty-four hours would be a fantasy come true. "All right," she said, standing up. "It's a deal."

With that, Claire started off down the hill. A few seconds later, Will caught up to her, the blanket tossed over his shoulder. He grabbed her hand, helping her navigate in the slippery grass. "Just so we're clear here, you're going to have power over me. Just me. None of the other blokes on Trall, right?"

"Gosh, I don't know," Claire teased. "If I dance well enough, I might just find myself a whole harem of men to please me."

He grabbed her hand and pulled her to a stop, then spun her around to face him. A moment later, his mouth came down on hers, drawing her into a deep, mind-numbing kiss. When he was finished, he stepped back. Claire glanced around and saw they'd distracted the crowd from Sorcha's dancing. "I'm the only bloke who'll be pleasing you here. Understood?"

Claire drew a ragged breath at the fierce look in his eyes. What had begun as a playful contest between them had suddenly turned serious. He'd made it clear how much he wanted her with every kiss and every caress. But this was different. It was as if he were claiming her body as his alone. "Promise?"

A smile touched his lips. "Yeah."

She turned and hurried down to the stone circle. As she moved through the crowd, some of her acquaintances from the town shouted out greetings and she waved—Beatrice Fraser and Annie Mulroony were standing together, and Billy Boyle was there. Claire found it odd that she'd been on Trall for four days and she was already treated like she'd lived there her entire life. It would be difficult to go back to the cold, impersonal atmosphere of Chicago.

Sorcha spotted her as she came into the light from one of the bonfires and she hurried over. "Join us!" she cried. She grabbed a holly garland from one of the passing dancers and placed it on Claire's head, then gave her a basket filled with grain. "Every now and again, toss some into the fire."

Claire glanced up at the hillside, but it was impossible to make out details of the crowd in the dark. She wasn't sure where Will was, but she could sense his eyes watching her. She followed Sorcha and tossed a handful of grain into the flames. It snapped and popped, sending sparks into the sky.

For a while, Claire just followed the line of women as they circled the altar and the fires. But soon, the music began to affect her. She tossed aside her hat and scarf and slipped out of her jacket, then began to move to the primal rhythm of the drum.

It was exhilarating and liberating and frightening all at once, and the more she danced, the more alive she felt. She closed her eyes and turned her face up to the sky as she twirled around, her hair falling over her eyes. Slowly, all her inhibitions dropped away and she felt a wonderful sense of freedom, as if all of her troubles had suddenly taken flight—Eric, her job, her future, nothing mattered anymore. She was here, in the present, and it was wonderful.

When she reached the back of thc circle, Claire stepped out of the line of dancers and leaned back against one of the stone pillars, taking a break from the action to watch the show. Her cheeks were cold and her breath clouded in front of her face. She closed her eyes and laughed at the craziness of it all. She did feel powerful.

Claire pushed away from the pillar, ready to join the dance again, but a hand grabbed her from behind and pulled her backward. She screamed, the sound covered by the chaos around her and a few seconds later, she was pressed up against the back of the pillar, hidden by the shadows.

The scent of him was already familiar to hcr and she sighed as Will kissed her, his body leaning into hers, his hands skimming along her torso. "Have I fulfilled my side of the deal already?" Claire asked as he nuzzled his face into her neck.

He didn't speak as his hands continued to roam over her body. When he slipped beneath her sweater, Claire held her breath, his cold fingers dancing against her warm skin. Though the activity in the stone circle was reaching a fever pitch, the drums beating faster, they were alone in the shadows, hidden by the pillar, unseen by the crowd on the other side of the circle.

He kissed her again, this time more gently, his tongue parting her lips. He was intent on seducing her, Claire could tell. And the prospect was even more exciting, here in the midst of the Samhain celebrations.

"I can't get close enough to you," he murmured, his tone desperate as he rubbed his hips against hers.

Claire felt the same way, caught up in an overwhelming need to touch him, to make him moan with pleasure. She reached for his belt and undid it, then fumbled with the zipper of his jeans. When she'd finally freed him, Claire wrapped her fingers around his hard shaft.

He whispered her name, his breath warm against her ear, then urged her on, telling her how good her touch felt. The sounds of the ceremony seemed to fade into the distance, a haze of passion surrounding them both. Claire was aware that they might be seen, but the night was black and they were alone.

Will slid down along her body and kissed her belly, then moved up until he'd bunched all her layers over her breasts. A moment later, his lips closed over her nipple and he sucked gently, bringing it to a peak. Claire was desperate for his touch, for the feel of his mouth on her skin. She raked her hands through his hair and guided him to her other nipple, crying out softly as he took it between his lips.

Her pulse pounded in rhythm with the drums and she drew him back up to her mouth, losing herself in a long, deep kiss. Will reached for the button on her jeans, but then ignored it and slipped his hand inside. He found the spot and touched her gently.

His caress sent a wave of pleasure coursing through

her and Claire was stunned at how aroused she'd become. She unzipped her jeans and Will slid them down along her hips as he continued to touch her.

It was all so primal, like the music and the dancing, all about instinct and pleasure. She wasn't afraid they'd be discovered and didn't care if they were. Her need for Will, for his touch and his taste, had taken control. But as she drew closer to her release, it wasn't enough.

They'd done this before, but this time, she wanted him inside her, if only for a few moments. "Make love to me," she murmured. "Now. Please. I need you."

He drew back, cupping her face and looking into her eyes. She could barely see him in the dark, but she sensed his uncertainty. "Are you sure?"

"Yes," she said.

Claire skimmed off her jeans and her panties, then shivered. Will grabbed the blanket from the ground and wrapped it around them both, providing her with a bit of modesty in case they were discovered.

A moment later, he handed her a condom—retrieved from his wallet—and she quickly smoothed it over his hard shaft. Then Will pressed her back against the stone pillar and drew her legs up around his waist.

Claire held her breath as he slid against her damp entrance. And then, he slowly brought her down onto him, sinking into her, inch by inch, until he was buried deep. For a long time he didn't move, his forehead pressed against her chest, her arms wrapped around his neck.

The length of him, filling her completely, brought a delicious sense of power and she arched against him, driving him even deeper. Will began to move then, slowly at first, as if he were already teetering on the edge. But neither one of them wanted to hold back.

He drove into her, again and again, Claire crying out with the pleasure, the sounds swallowed by the night and the noise of the crowd. He shifted her in his arms and suddenly, he moved against her in a different way…a way that brought a flood of pleasure.

"Oh," she moaned. "Oh, please." Claire felt her desire heighten and then, to her surprise, she dissolved into a powerful orgasm. Her body convulsed around him and a moment later, he joined her, burying himself more deeply than before.

It was over as quickly as it had begun, but for Claire, it had been the most passionate sex she'd ever experienced. Will's knees seemed to buckle beneath him and he slowly lowered her to the ground until she sat on her discarded jeans. He sat down next to her, his back against the stone pillar, and she covered them both with the blanket.

"Wow," she said, closing eyes and smiling.

"Yeah," he said. He drew a shaky breath. "Well put. Wow."

"I've never done anything quite like that," Claire said.

"Neither have I." He slipped his arm around her shoulders and pulled her against his body. Claire barely felt the cold. Her body still trembled with the power of her orgasm and the impact of what they'd shared.

"We should go," he said. "We can continue this in my bed."

Claire glanced at him. "You're supposed to be my slave for the night, aren't you?"

He stood up and, taking her hand, he helped her to her feet, then steadied her as she got dressed. They found her jacket, hat and scarf and then walked back to Will's Range Rover, hand in hand, the blanket wrapped around their shoulders. Will helped her inside, then jogged around, hopping in behind the wheel. But before he started the truck, he leaned over and kissed her again, softly and sweetly, his hands cupping her face.

"You were beautiful out there, dancing in the firelight. I've never seen anything quite so lovely."

Claire felt her cheeks warm with a blush. "Thank you."

Will started the Range Rover and Claire stretched her legs out. Her feet bumped up against something and it rolled away. Claire reached down and picked up the water bottle she'd refilled at the Druid spring that afternoon. When she delivered Sorcha's boxes, she'd noticed that the bottle was empty and the cap loose. So on her way back to the inn, she'd driven to the spring to refill it.

Claire tucked the bottle beneath her leg and glanced over at Will, whose attention was focused on weaving through the cars that were parked along the lane. Her fingers tightened on the bottle and she pulled it out and removed the cap.

Drawing a deep breath, she held it out to him. "Would you like a drink?" she asked.

He glanced over at her and smiled. "Sure," he said, taking the bottle from her. "Thanks."

Will took a long swig of the water, then handed it back to her. Claire took a sip and replaced the top, her fingers trembling slightly. If the water really did work, then she'd just made a very important choice in giving it to Will.

All of her reasons for coming to Trall had been put aside. All of her dreams for the future were now forgotten. She wanted Will. And whether it was for a day, a week or a lifetime, she didn't care.

CLAIRE SNUGGLED beneath the down comforter on Will's bed, pulling it over her head to block out the morning light. Will had crawled out of bed at sunrise and headed to the kitchen to help Katie with breakfast. He'd promised to return when the guests had been fed, but it was nearly ten and he was still gone.

Claire sat up and brushed her tangled hair out of her eyes. They'd come home from the stone circle and gone right to his room, stripping off their clothes and climbing into bed. But they'd spent most of the night talking, wrapped in each others' embrace, limbs tangled, breath mingled.

Families, lovers, jobs, childhood memories. They covered it all. An hour before the sun came up, Will made love to her again, slowly and patiently, as if he were savoring every sensation and allowing her to do the same. And the orgasm they had shared was sweet and warm and full of longing.

Impatient to see him, Claire rolled out of bed and gathered her clothes from the floor, tugging them on as she retrieved them. When she was dressed, she splashed some cold water on her face, took a gulp of Will's mouthwash and ran his comb through her hair.

She walked through the parlor and then carefully

opened the door into the kitchen. She saw him standing over the sink, rinsing dishes. Claire tiptoed through the quiet kitchen, then wrapped her arms around his waist from behind. "Good morning," she said.

Will stiffened slightly. "You're up," he said.

His voice was cool and Claire frowned. "I thought you were going to come back to bed." She stepped around him to stand at the counter, leaning back against the edge so that she might look up at his face. He didn't look at her, instead keeping his eyes fixed on his task.

"We have a new guest," he said. "I was getting him settled." He finally did look at Claire and she saw a flash of anger in his eyes. "You'll be interested to know, he's from Chicago. Or was, until recently. In fact, you know him."

Claire swallowed hard. "Eric?" she asked.

"The one and only," Will said. "He's out there having breakfast. He's already been up to your room. I told him you'd gone out for a walk this morning and hadn't returned. I didn't think you'd want him to discover you, naked, in my bed."

"I don't want to see him," Claire said. "Go out there and tell him you were mistaken. Tell him I left on the ferry this morning."

"He came over on the ferry this morning. He would have run into you if you'd been getting off on the mainland."

"We broke up via a Post-it," she said.

"What?"

"You know, a little green sticky note, stuck on my bathroom mirror."

"Coward," Will muttered.

"I'm not going to talk to him," Claire said. "Nothing he says will make any difference."

"Maybe you ought to tell him that to his face?" Will suggested.

"No. If I ignore him, he'll go away."

"He's staying," Will said. "He took a room."

Claire gasped. "You gave him a room? Why would you do something like that?"

"Because he asked for one. And I didn't know who the hell he was until he signed the register and asked for you." Will stepped away from the sink and grabbed a dishrag, then dried his hands and tossed it aside. "I have to go to the market. I'll be back in an hour."

"Will, I didn't invite him here. And I'm not happy that he's come." Claire grabbed his hands and looked up into his eyes. It was clear he was irritated by Eric's arrival, but he was keeping his anger in check. "I'll get rid of him. I promise."

Will shrugged. "You don't need to make me any promises, Claire," he murmured.

Claire pushed up on her toes and brushed a kiss across his lips. At first, she thought that would be the end of it. But then Will furrowed his hands through her hair and molded her mouth to his, capturing her in a fierce and frantic kiss. When he was finished, he gave her a tight smile, then grabbed his jacket and walked out the back door.

She closed her eyes, suddenly aware of a growing headache. The last person in the world she wanted to see was Eric. There was nothing to say. She'd moved on. Over the past four days and three nights, she'd managed to completely get over the man she'd lived with for three years.

Claire rubbed her eyes. How was that possible? Eric had been her life, her future, and now she couldn't even remember why she'd been in love with him. Perhaps it was a good idea to talk to him, to put an end to it once and for all.

She walked through the butler's pantry and peered through the crack in the door to the dining room. The room was empty except for a pair of elderly women sipping at their tea in the corner. Eric was reading a newspaper at a table near the window. His back was to her as she approached and Claire silently slipped into the chair across from him.

He lowered the newspaper. "Claire," he intoned as if they'd just seen each other an hour before.

"What are you doing here?" she whispered.

"You look good," he said.

Claire glanced over at the ladies, but they were deep in their own conversation. "Don't you start with that. Don't try to sweet-talk me. Answer my question. Why are you here?"

"I came here to apologize."

Claire laughed. "You came all the way to Ireland to apologize? You could have sent me a letter. Or better yet, a Post-it note."

He drew a deep breath. "The truth is, I need you," he said.

"It's a little late for that," Claire snapped back. "If you think I'm ever going to sleep with you a—"

"Not that way. Professionally. I just started work with a big agency in Manhattan and I'm managing their newest account, a major airline. The art director is a complete incompetent and if I don't find someone to replace him, we're doomed. You worked with me on MidAmerican Air and you did a wonderful job, Claire. I need you to come to New York and work with me again."

Claire stared at him in disbelief. He'd come all this way to offer her a job? "Then you didn't come here to—"

"I won't say that I haven't been thinking about you. And that I may have handled things badly."

"You won't say that?" Claire asked.

"All right, I'll say it. I've been thinking about you and I'm sorry for the way I handled things. I was a shit and you have every right to hate me. But I want to make it up to you. The agency will pay for your move to New York. They'll double your salary and help find you an apartment. This is a big step, Claire. There's a lot riding on me putting together a good team. And if there are any bad feelings between us, then this won't work."

A giggle burst from Claire's throat. "Bad feelings? You're a spineless worm who didn't have the decency to be honest with me."

Eric took a deep breath and nodded. "All right, I can respect that. But those feelings aside, I still think we can work together." He reached out and covered her hand with his. "And who knows, maybe we'll get the rest of it back on track, too."

"No!" Claire said, slapping his hand. She stood up and punched his shoulder, hard. He winced and she took some satisfaction in that. "Go home, Eric."

"Just think about it, Claire. This would be a huge career move for you."

She stepped back, her chair screeching across the hardwood floor of the dining room. The two ladies glanced their way and Claire pasted a smile on her face. "Go home," she said.

"I won't until you've considered my offer. Take some time, cool down, and think about how much this would mean for you."

She shook her head, then frowned. "How did you know I was here?"

"Your grandmother. I was surprised. Why Ireland? And why this island in the middle of nowhere? Do you know how difficult it was to get here? There's no airport. I had to take a boat."

"Poor you," Claire said. "All that hassle for nothing." With that, she spun on her heel and walked out of the dining room. When she reached the stairs, she took them two at a time. By the time she reached her own room, Claire's eyes were swimming with tears.

Why had he come here? He'd ruined everything. She and Will were just beginning to truly know each other and now she was left to explain this all to him. Claire sank down on the edge of the bed and covered her eyes with her hands.

Though Eric wasn't her favorite person right now, she couldn't deny that his bad behavior had sent her here—and here is where she'd found Will Donovan. A shiver coursed through her as she thought of Will, lying naked beside her in his bed, his hair tousled, his body completely relaxed. He was the man she wanted now, not Eric.

She'd secretly allowed herself to imagine a life on this island with Will. She'd help him run the inn and in her spare time, she'd paint. Claire had always wanted to take up painting again and there were so many beautiful places on Trall to inspire her. But counting on a future with Will was silly at best. They'd known each other for four days.

And she'd never even considered leaving Chicago until now. Her entire family was there, her parents, her brothers and their families, and her grandmother. A move to New York would be an agonizing choice, but if she lived in Ireland, then she might as well live on the moon.

Still, there were practical matters to consider. Although Will offered incredible passion, that didn't pay the bills. The job Eric offered was a future, the kind of career that she'd always dreamed about. Working for an agency in Manhattan would put her in the middle of the creative universe. She'd live in a city that offered the best in theatre and museums and shopping and restaurants. She'd meet new people and make new friends. And she'd have enough money and time to fly home once a month. Two hours by plane was a quick trip.

Claire sighed. Her life could get back on track. That's what Eric had said about their relationship. "Back on track," she murmured. But what track? The one that led to a boring existence with a man who barely had time for her? Or the one that led to a life of excitement and passion and happiness with a man who made her heart beat faster every time she saw him?

She and Eric had been on the wrong track. Her time

with Will had proved that. Deep in her heart, she knew Will would always be the standard of measure when it came to desire. Every man who came after him would always fall short, and that frightened Claire, for she knew that from now on, every minute that passed was one more than what she had left.

But desire faded. Hadn't her relationship with Eric proved that point? The end to this vacation fantasy was coming and she would have to go home. At least, if she accepted Eric's offer, she'd have something to go home to.

WILL THREW OPEN the front door of Sorcha's shop and strode inside. He knew she'd be around, catching the last of the tourist trade before they left the island for home. "Sorcha!" he shouted.

A moment later, she emerged from behind a curtained doorway. Her red hair was rumpled and it looked as if she hadn't bothered to comb it that morning. She was wearing a long flowing dress and bracelets that jangled as she walked. "Will! Good morning. I'm sorry, but weren't we going to go pick up my things later this afternoon?"

"Right," Will said. "I forgot. Hell, drop by the inn and I'll give you the keys to the Range Rover. Whenever you're ready."

She frowned. "Are you all right?"

"Yes," Will muttered. "No. No. I'm not. I need your help."

Sorcha blinked in surprise. "With what?"

"Magic."

A slow smile curved her lips and her eyes sparkled in delight. "Oh, Will, this is quite unexpected. But I suppose I shouldn't be surprised. It was clear to everyone with eyes that you and the American are gagging for each other. You kissed her in front of God and all of Trall. Everyone's talking about it." Sorcha pulled up a stool and sat down behind the counter. "I must say, Will, she's a lovely girl. I've grown fond of her and I think you two make a fine pair."

"Thank you," Will said.

"And I'm not sure I could, in good conscience, sell you magic that would increase her desire for you. I like Claire and I wouldn't want to trick her. I've removed all the spells. And she's asked me for the water, but I've refused to give it to her. You're on your own."

"I wouldn't want you to trick her," Will said. "I need the magic for her fiancé. Actually, her ex-fiancé. He showed up this morning and I think he's going to convince her to go home with him. I want him stopped."

"You really are smitten with her."

"I am. But it's only been four days and I have no idea how she really feels. If she leaves, we'll never know."

Sorcha rested her chin in her palm and studied him intently. "So, is the sex fabulous? Is that why you want her to stay?"

"Didn't we decide that my sex life was none of your business?"

"I'm asking on a purely professional level, Will. Consider me your therapist, of sorts. You can confide in me."

"So you can have the details broadcast over the

entire island by sundown? No. Suffice it to say that everything between us was going smoothly until this bloke dropped in."

Sorcha frowned. "Well, I have any number of spells I could perform, depending upon your desired result."

"I was thinking more about your own personal magic. That thing you do to men. You know, that… thing." Will cleared his throat. "You might like this guy. He's decent-looking, he's successful, he seems friendly enough. He might be worth a look."

"You want me to shag him?" Sorcha asked.

Will scoffed. "No. I just want you to occupy him. Flirt, tempt, do what you do best. Enthrall him until I have time to figure out whether Claire is still in love with him." Will rubbed his hands together. "I'm going to ask Claire to go to the mainland with me. I'll make up some excuse, but we'll spend the night. That will give you time to figure out what this Eric is up to."

Sorcha considered the proposition for a long moment. "What do I get out of this?"

"What do you want?"

"Oh, you are a desperate man. And you've put me on the spot. I'm not sure what I want. But it will be something big. Something very big."

"Whatever you want, it's yours."

"Oh, I know. I want your bed!"

"Why? You've never slept in it."

"I like it. It looks like it was made for a Druid priestess."

"All right. But only if I convince Claire to stay on the island."

"Forever? That's a fool's bet. Why would she want to stay on Trall?"

"For a month. Then, you can have the bed."

Sorcha considered the deal, then nodded and held out her hand. "Done," she said as Will shook on it.

"Katie is going to take care of the inn while I'm gone. But I want you to drop by and meet our newest guest. You can spend the night. Just find any empty room. You've got forty-eight hours, Sorcha. Do your magic."

She tossed her red hair back over her shoulders. "A handsome single man on Trall. You did say he was handsome, didn't you?"

"I'm not the best judge of these things, but yes, I'd say he was handsome. And tall. And very American."

"I've never had an American before. I suppose I owe it to myself to at least give him a go."

"What you decide to do with him is entirely up to you." Will started for the door, then turned back and smiled at Sorcha. "No, that's not right. I don't want you hurt. And I know you aren't as cavalier about sex as you lead everyone to believe. Just flirt with him a little, Sorcha. Distract him. Buy me some time."

Sorcha returned his smile. "I can do that," she said. "Now, be off with you. I'll pop over to the inn as soon as I close the shop."

Will stepped out onto the street and headed back to the Range Rover. He'd finished the marketing for the next three days and he had a few things to tidy up at the inn before he'd be able to leave. If he could tempt Claire to accompany him, then maybe he'd have a chance. But a chance for what?

There was no denying he'd enjoyed the past four days and that the sex had been incredible. But what did he really want from her? Had it been so long that he was fabricating some future for himself? She was a beautiful woman and their attraction was intense. But was there anything beyond that?

Desire could blind a man to the realities of relationships. It had happened in the past, although he'd never felt this level of need for a woman before. There wasn't a minute that passed where he didn't think about her, about them, together. And his thoughts, though detailed and quite graphic, still weren't as good as the real thing.

Claire was a woman who had managed to make his fantasies much better in real life than they were in his head. His mind wandered back to the previous evening, to their encounter against the stone pillar. He'd never done anything in his life quite like that. The danger of discovery mixed with the passion of possessing her was intoxicating. And the resulting orgasm was powerful. He needed to believe that he'd experience it all again. With Claire.

When Will reached the inn, he jumped out of the truck and strode to the front door. He half expected Claire and her fiancé to be snuggled up in the parlor in front of the fire. But the main floor was empty. He walked back to the kitchen and found Katie scrubbing a skillet she'd used for breakfast.

"Everything all right?" Will asked.

She nodded, a cheery smile on her face. "The American bloke is out back talking on his mobile. And Miss O'Connor is still upstairs. The two spinsters from

Nottingham are having a walk around the island and the couple from Scotland decided to get lunch in town."

"I'm going over to the mainland on the one p.m. car ferry. I need you to watch over the inn for the next few days. If you need help, call Sorcha. She'll stop by this evening. Once the guests leave tomorrow morning, there's no one scheduled to arrive until next weekend so you can lock the doors."

Katie nodded. "Take your mobile so I can ring you if I have any problems."

Will nodded, giving her a grateful smile, then turned and headed out to the entry hall. Once he had Claire off the island and out of her ex's reach, he could figure out how he really felt about her. But as he jogged up the stairs, Will couldn't help but wonder if he already knew how he felt and was just afraid to admit it.

6

CLAIRE STARED UP at the ceiling above her bed, trying to make outlines of animals from the cracks in the plaster. She'd been hiding out for most of the morning and early afternoon in an effort to avoid another conversation with Eric. She'd showered, shaved her legs, painted her fingernails and toenails, and plucked her eyebrows. There was nothing left to do now but stare at the ceiling.

Why had he come? He should have known she didn't want to see him. And what could have possibly convinced him she'd consider working in the same office as him? Sure, she might have come all the way to Ireland in an attempt to save their relationship, but that could be written off as a hysterical reaction to a really awful time in her life.

Now that she'd had a chance to calm down and gain some perspective on the matter, she realized that the last person she wanted in her life was Eric. Claire groaned and flipped over on her stomach, burying her face in the down pillow. But that didn't bring her any sense of closure. Instead, she was left to face the new dilemma in her life—Will Donovan.

How had her life spun so wildly out of control? She'd always planned so carefully, measuring every step, weighing each option and only making a move when she knew it would result in her future happiness.

Falling into bed with Will was supposed to have been just a bit of naughty fun, a thrill she might never have the chance to experience again. She'd been so certain she could walk away without any regrets. And now that the time was approaching, Claire realized it would be impossible to leave Ireland without a suitcase full of doubts and regrets.

On reflection, Eric's offer *would* give her a start to a new plan. But what exactly did he expect from her? Claire wasn't sure she wanted to know the answer. Maybe it was just best to avoid the question entirely.

A soft knock sounded on the door and Claire jumped off the bed. "Go away, Eric," she called. "I don't want to talk to you."

"It's Will."

A flood of relief washed over her. Claire pulled the door open and dragged Will inside, then shut the door behind him. "Is he still downstairs?"

"He just left. He was going to walk into town and get some lunch. He asked that I give you this when you came down." Will held out a small box.

"What is it?" Claire asked.

He shrugged. "I don't know. I didn't open it and I didn't bother to ask."

His voice was cold, his manner aloof. This was not the same funny, affectionate man she'd fallen into bed with just last night, the same intensely passionate man who'd made love to her against a stone pillar. "I—I didn't ask him to come here," Claire said. "I don't want him here."

Will's jaw was set, his lips pressed into a tight line. "Then tell him to go home."

She hesitated and then saw the instant look of suspicion in Will's eyes. "He's offered me a job. And I'm not sure I shouldn't take it. It's with a big agency in New York."

"Sounds like a great opportunity. You should take it."

"You don't sound convincing," Claire teased, hoping to get a smile out of him. She tossed the box on the bed.

"Aren't you going to open it?"

Claire shook her head. "I don't care what's inside, it wouldn't make a difference."

Will reached across the bed and grabbed the box, then handed it to her. "Open it."

She sighed, knowing that he wouldn't be satisfied until she did. Claire pulled the lid off the box, then froze. Inside was a small velvet bag with the name of a famous Chicago jeweler embroidered across the front in gold thread. "I don't need to open it."

Will grabbed the bag and loosened the drawstring, then reached inside. He pulled out a beautiful sapphire ring, the blue stone surrounded by tiny diamonds. "Well, this will go a long way toward making up for that note he left on the mirror."

Claire stared at the ring. "He was going to propose."

Will grabbed her hand and pushed the ring onto her finger. "Is this what you want? Because if it is, then fine. But if this guy dumped you the way you said he did, then you're a bloody eedjit to even consider his offer. You deserve better. Much better."

"I don't want him," Claire said, tugging the ring off her finger and sticking it back into the bag. "But I have to consider the job offer. I don't have an endless supply of money. In another few months, I won't have a home. What am I going to do? Stay here with you?"

The moment she said the words, Claire wanted to take them back. Or perhaps rephrase them so they didn't sound so sarcastic. In truth, it would be so simple to stay with Will, to continue on as they'd begun. But she knew their attraction was based simply on lust and not on anything more substantial.

After a time, the desire would fade and they'd both be left to realize they were different people from different worlds, with absolutely nothing in common. "I'm sorry," she murmured. "You've been nothing but kind and generous to me. And I don't want you to think I haven't enjoyed every minute we've—"

"Don't," he said, holding up his hand. Will glanced around the room, then walked over to the closet and retrieved her bag. "Come on," he said. "We're going to get out of here. Pack enough for a day or two."

Claire frowned. "Where are we going?"

"I don't know. But we're going to get off this island. Away from your fiancé."

"He was never my fiancé," Claire reminded him. "Not technically."

"When you're packed, come down the servants' stairs. The door is at the far end of the hallway. It opens into the kitchen. We'll sneak out the back."

"You can't just leave. You have guests."

"I leave all the time," Will said, opening the top drawer of her dresser and grabbing a handful of her underwear. He handed it to her. "Katie is going to stay and watch the inn."

Deep inside, Claire knew she ought to refuse. Already, it would be painfully difficult to leave Ireland. Spending more time with Will couldn't possibly make it easier. But she was willing to accept the consequences for just a few more nights alone with him. "All right," she said.

Will grabbed her and kissed her, long and hard. He drew back and smoothed a strand of hair from her face, then touched the tip of her nose with his lips. She saw the look in his eyes, the anger slowly giving way to relief, the tension in his jaw relaxing.

A shiver ran down Claire's spine as she remembered the sensation of him moving inside of her. They would share that again. Tonight. She smoothed her hand over his chest, her fingers skimming along hard muscle beneath soft fabric. "Give me a minute," she said. "I'll finish packing and come right down."

"Hurry. We need to make the last ferry."

When the door closed behind him, Claire pressed her hand to her heart. It pounded beneath her palm. How was it possible that this man could make her feel so alive just by touching her? Was there really magic at work here?

She turned back to the bed and finished packing, her anticipation growing with each item of clothing she threw into the bag. Then she stripped off the silk robe she'd put on after her shower and pulled out a pair of jeans and a clingy long-sleeved T-shirt. The shirt was cut low in front, offering a tempting view of the tops of her breasts. Claire picked out a sexy black bra and thong to go beneath. "It always pays to be prepared," she murmured to herself, smiling.

They would spend the night together, in the same bed. And given those circumstances, things were bound to happen. She was simply going to make sure she looked her best. She quickly slipped on her shoes, zipped the bag and grabbed her jacket.

Claire peeked out the door before she stepped into the hallway. She found the servants' stairs and tiptoed down to the kitchen. He was waiting there, car keys in hand.

"Ready?" he asked.

Claire handed him her bag. "Where are we going?"

He gave her a smile, the first smile she'd seen since Eric had arrived. "It's a surprise."

"Will it involve a Druid ceremony and outdoor sex?" she asked. "I'm willing to be the sacrificial virgin."

Will pulled the back door open and ushered her outside. "I thought we'd already established the fact that you weren't a virgin."

"There are different types of virgins. I'd never had sex outdoors until last night, so I suppose I did qualify in one way."

Will helped her into the Mercedes, then bent over the door. "Interesting. And what other things haven't you done?"

Claire glanced up at him from beneath her lashes. "Lots of things. You want a list or should I just let you know when we get to them?"

He chuckled softly, then closed the car door. A few minutes later, they were racing down the road into town. They made the ferry with just a few minutes to spare, driving onto the flat-decked boat to join the three other cars onboard.

Claire remembered her trip out to Trall in the small mail boat, how she'd come full of emotion, determined to find a way to put her relationship with Eric back together again. And now, she was running away from him, to be with another man.

As the ferry began to pull away from the landing, Will hopped out of the car and came around to open Claire's door. He put his arm around her shoulders and they walked to the stern of the boat and watched as the island faded into the distance.

"What was it about him that you loved?" Will asked.

Claire glanced up at him. He continued to stare at the horizon, the breeze buffeting his hair, his lips slightly parted. "I made this list when I was younger. Of all the things I wanted in a man. And he fit the list. So I fell in love with him. But, now, I'm not sure that I didn't just convince myself I loved him because he fit the list."

"What was on the list?"

"The usual stuff. Tall, handsome, well-educated, clever, driven professionally, good prospects. Up until a week ago, I thought I had everything I could possibly want."

Will turned to her, slipping his arms around her waist. "And now?"

"I have no idea what I want. And it scares me a little."

He pulled her body against his and kissed her

forehead. "It's not always necessary to have a plan," he said. "Sometimes, you just have to let life happen."

"Is that what we're doing?" Claire asked.

"As best as I can tell," Will answered. He chuckled softly. "If we're going to engage in such serious conversation, then this is bound to be a dull trip."

"And what are you going to do to make it exciting?" Claire countered.

"I have plenty of ideas," he said. He leaned close as if to whisper something in Claire's ear. But instead, he nibbled at it gently. "We'll get to all of that later. I promise."

THE FERRY LANDED at the tiny harbor town of Fermoy, on the Dingle Peninsula. It was nearly dark by the time Will drove the car onto the landing. "I'm afraid you won't be seeing much along the way," he said. "But I promise to show you some sights tomorrow."

"I wasn't paying much attention when I arrived," she said. "I was exhausted and worried about getting to the island. I didn't even notice the scenery passing by on the way from the airport. Where are we going?"

"It's not far," Will said.

"I'm famished. I was afraid to go downstairs to get some lunch, so I haven't had a bite to eat all day."

"There'll be dinner where we're going," he said.

Will knew the roads by heart, knew exactly how long it took to get from the ferry landing to the small village of Castlemaine and then to the old stone house on the River Maine. When he pulled into the drive, he was happy to see that the lights had been turned on.

"This is lovely," Claire said, staring out the window.

"I'm glad you like it."

He parked the car and they walked to the front door. Will punched the security code into the keypad and after the lock clicked, he opened the door for Claire. The house had been closed up for three months, but the caretaker had managed to take the chill out of the air with a cozy fire in the front parlor. With the exception of the parlor, the rooms on the main floor were empty of furniture, sold over the past few years as Will divested himself of his former life.

Claire frowned. "Are we staying here?"

Will nodded. "This is my house. It's not much, but it's cozy and we have everything we need here. There's a bedroom on the second floor that's still furnished and the kitchen is stocked."

"This is your house?" She slowly began to wander through the rooms, turning on lights along the way. Will had bought the old manor house after he'd made his first million. And he'd spent another million restoring it and furnishing it.

"You lived here?" Claire asked.

"I still do on occasion. When I have work in Killarney. There was furniture here at one time. I've just sold it off, bit by bit. My business manager thought the house would be a good investment. I rent it out now. For parties, sometimes for weddings. The grounds are beautiful. The river is just out back. They've shot a couple of movies here and a BBC program."

Claire stared up at the crystal chandelier in the dining room. "It's odd," she murmured. "It doesn't really seem like you."

He laughed. "I thought this was what I wanted," he said. "What I needed to show everyone how successful I was, to prove that I'd made enough money to afford something this grand. But then I moved in here and it was so big and empty. Kind of like a metaphor for my life."

"But you were successful," Claire said.

"I'm not sure success is supposed to come so quickly. I was twenty-five years old. When it does, it doesn't seem real. All the money and the things that money buys, it's supposed to make a person happy. It only made me…disillusioned and I couldn't understand why."

"You made all of this inventing a computer program?" Claire smiled. "Annie Mulroony told me. She said it wasn't gossip since it had been printed in all the papers."

"Computer software. And I was at the right place at the right time with the right product."

"It must have been more than luck."

"I developed a new kind of facial recognition software. It extrapolated a two-dimensional photo into a three-dimension data set. So it could recognize faces from different angles. It was right at the time when airports were stepping up security and governments were creating watch lists. I had what they needed and they were more than willing to pay."

Claire continued her tour, through the butler's pantry and into the kitchen. Will opened the refrigerator and began to pull out cartons. As ordered, the caretaker had brought in supper for them both from Will's favorite restaurant in Killarney. He'd also pulled a bottle of champagne from the wine cellar and put it in the refrigerator for them.

Will grabbed a pair of flutes from the cabinet, and the bottle of champagne, and walked over to the table in the breakfast room. "Dinner is takeaway," he said. "But we've got very good champagne." He popped the cork and filled a glass for Claire, then handed it to her.

"We're completely alone here?" she asked.

Will nodded. "Completely."

Claire shrugged out of her jacket and let it drop to the floor, then kicked off her shoes. Will felt a warm flood of desire race through his bloodstream. He liked having Claire in this house, in his house. Odd, Will mused. He'd never been completely comfortable here, until now.

He took off his own jacket and tossed it over the back of a chair. "Should we have a toast then?"

Claire nodded.

He held up his glass. "May you live as long as you want and never want as long as you live," Will declared. He touched his glass to Claire's, then took a sip of the champagne. "If you don't like champagne, I'm sure I could find what's needed for chocolate martinis."

Claire groaned. "I'll never drink them again. Although it wasn't the martinis. It was the drinking game we were playing. It seemed like I was always the one drinking."

"What game did you play?"

"'I Never.' It's funny, because I shouldn't have lost. But they kept picking things that I hadn't done. And then I had to drink."

"Sorcha cheats," Will said. "And that's not the way

you play the game. One person says something they've never done and if you've done it, then you have to take a drink. That's how the game goes. Like when you said you'd never made love outdoors. If I have, then I'd have to drink."

"And have you?" Claire asked.

Will shook his head. "Well, if you don't count my messing about during my teenage years, last night was my first time, too."

"Interesting," she murmured. "This is a very good way to get to know each other. I think we should play."

"You want to play now? Maybe we should have some dinner first," he suggested. "Drinking champagne on an empty stomach might not be the best thing."

"All right, I'll start," Claire said. "I never jumped out of a plane."

"I haven't, either," Will said. "So I don't have to drink. I've never…climbed a mountain."

Claire frowned and took a sip of her champagne. "Eric dragged me up some mountain in Colorado. I hated every minute of it. I've never…been to France."

This time Will took a sip. "I've never…known a woman quite as beautiful as you."

Claire laughed. "Now that's very clever. If I don't drink, then it makes me look like I'm full of myself. And if I do, it makes me look like I don't think I'm pretty."

"You are pretty." It wasn't difficult to say the words. They were true, Will mused.

"But I know a lot of other women who are prettier. I think I'm going to have to take a big drink with that." She took a long swallow and smiled.

"I don't," Will said, taking a long sip as well. "I don't know any women who are prettier than you."

Claire smiled at him and Will felt his blood warm. There were times when he couldn't imagine wanting her more. And then she'd give him a look or a smile and Will would realize that his desire for her had no boundaries.

"That wasn't part of the game," she said, "but it was a nice thing to say." Claire paused to think of her next statement. "I've never made love in a kitchen. Almost, but never."

"Yesterday morning?" Will arched his eyebrow, then took a sip. "I think we can probably work on that some more. How about I've never licked champagne from a woman's breasts?"

Claire clapped her hand to her mouth in mock surprise. "Neither have I." She reached for the hem of her T-shirt and slowly pulled it over her head. "Why don't we fix that for you right now?" As she boosted herself up on the table, Will couldn't help but laugh. Claire lay down in front of him, her back arched slightly, her body his to admire. He reached for the front closure of her bra and unhooked it, the lacy black satin falling aside.

She took his glass of champagne and dribbled it over her breasts and belly. Growling softly, Will leaned over and began to lick it from her skin. Her flesh was soft and warm and she moaned as he circled her nipple with his tongue. Will moved on until all the champagne was gone.

"That's nice," she whispered. "For someone who has never done that before, you do it quite well."

"You're next," Will said. "You'd better make it good."

Claire sat up, bracing her hands behind her. "All right. I've never done a striptease for a man."

"I haven't, either," Will said. "I've never had a striptease done for me."

"I haven't, either," Claire said. "Maybe we could kill two 'I Nevers' with one striptease."

Claire giggled and slid off the table. She slipped out of her bra and tossed it in his face, humming a little tune as she improvised a dance. Though Will was supposed to participate, he found a much greater pleasure in watching. Was there nothing she wouldn't do to tantalize him?

She reached for the button of her jeans, then slowly drew the zipper down. "I'm not the only one getting naked here," she complained.

"But you're the only one worth watching," Will countered.

Claire reached for the hem of his shirt and pulled it up and over his head. "I beg to differ. If you worked in one of those ladies' clubs, you'd have hundred-dollar bills sticking out of your underwear. Now strip."

Will kicked off his shoes and socks, then slid his jeans over his hips. Claire stood back and clapped, then grabbed her purse and pulled out a euro note. She crooked her finger at him and he came closer, then she tucked the money into the front of his boxers.

Will grabbed her around the waist and pulled her up against him, kissing the curve of her neck. "I've never wanted a woman more than I wanted you," he said.

"I give up," Claire said. "You win. Game over."

"Do I get you as my prize?" Will asked.

"No," she said. "I get you."

Her mouth was as sweet from the champagne as her skin was and he drew his tongue along her lower lip until he'd licked the last taste away. His lips dropped to her shoulder, to skin so soft it felt like silk. She tilted her head and sighed as he explored the ridge of her collarbone and the notch at the base of her neck.

Every place he touched was perfect, soft and warm, made for his hands. He'd always been fascinated by the female body, but with Claire it had become an obsession to know every detail, every square inch of skin, every gentle curve. He wanted to be able to recall it all at a moment's notice, to know that she had been his completely.

He smoothed his palms across her back then slipped them beneath the waistband of her jeans. Will moaned when his fingers caught the elastic of her thong. It was obvious she'd chosen her underwear carefully.

Claire stepped back out of his embrace, then pressed her hand to his chest, pushing him back until he sat on the edge of the table. Then, with her gaze fixed to his, she continued her striptease.

Will held his breath as she slid her thumbs beneath the waistband of her jeans and ran them back and forth. She watched for his reaction and Will smiled, biting at his lower lip as he tried to keep his wits about him. He'd been seduced before, but it had never had this effect on him. He was already hard and aching for release, but yet, he wanted this slow foreplay to continue.

Claire turned her back to him, skimming the denim over her hips. Will released a tightly held breath as she bent forward. He wasn't sure how much more he could take of this. His fingers trembled with the need to touch her.

When she straightened, turned and stepped toward him, he reached out, but Claire took his hands and gently placed them on the edge of the table. Then she began to remove his boxers. Will didn't touch her, but instead gave himself over to her touch.

She ran her hands over his chest, teasing at his nipples with her fingernails until they were hard. Will sucked in a quick breath and then closed his eyes as her lips found one nipple, then the other. This was torture, he thought to himself. No matter where she touched him, it seemed to send a flood of desire coursing through his body. He ached with the need to come and was afraid that the moment she touched him there, it would all be over.

"Why are you doing this to me?" he muttered as she trailed kisses down his belly.

"Is there something else we should be doing? Maybe we should go back to the drinking game?"

"Oh, no," Will said.

"Then stop complaining," she said. She slowly stood, rubbing her body against his as she rose, her breasts warm against his skin, her belly soft against his erection. Will bent forward and kissed her shoulder. She trembled and he heard her teeth chatter. "You're cold," he breathed.

"No," she said.

"Yes." Will took her hand and led her to the front of the house, turning off the lights as they walked back to the parlor. He tossed more peat onto the fire, then he drew her closer and rubbed her arms. "Better?"

"Mmm," she said.

Will kissed the top of her head. "Wait here." He walked back to the foyer and grabbed his bag, then pulled out the box of condoms he'd brought along. Then he grabbed a cashmere throw from the back of the sofa and wrapped it around her shoulders.

"I haven't had a naked woman in this house, so I'm not really prepared," he teased, rubbing her arms. "We could go upstairs. There's a down comforter on the bed."

"I like it here," Claire said. "I've never made love in front of a fireplace." She knelt down on the floor, then grabbed his fingers and brought him down in front of her. Will smoothed his hands over her face, staring into her eyes and wondering how he'd ever do without this. In one short week, he'd become completely captivated by this woman, as if he'd fallen under some strange spell.

He'd tried to convince himself it was a momentary infatuation, a flame that would burn brightly but then fade. Instead, every moment they spent together seemed to increase his need. He didn't want hours or days with her. He wanted months and years, time enough to satisfy this hunger deep inside of him.

But if he had to let her go, then he would. And he would remember every perfect moment between them. Will captured her face between his hands and kissed her, lingering over her mouth. Is this what he'd been waiting for all this time?

They tumbled to the floor, Will stretching out alongside her on the soft oriental carpet. His hands tangled in her hair, shimmering like gold in the firelight. "Could you love me?" he whispered. "Just for tonight?"

A smile touched her lips and she reached out and ran a finger along his jawline. "I love you," she said. "Just for tonight."

And when he entered her and began to move, Will let her words drive him forward. For tonight, she loved him. And what they shared was no longer just sex. It had become a deeper emotional connection. And for the first time in his adult life, the emptiness inside of him began to disappear, the space filled with the scent of her and the feel of her, and the need to possess her. She had changed him forever and Will wasn't sure he could let that go.

CLAIRE HAD VACATIONED in many beautiful locations, but as she stood on a rise overlooking Lough Learie, she couldn't remember ever seeing a more beautiful place.

A haze rose from the water, softening the landscape until it looked like a watercolor painting. Every now and then, the sun would break through the clouds and send shafts of light onto the lake and the surrounding trees, making the colors even more brilliant.

"Do you ever get used to this?" she asked.

"What do you mean?" Will countered.

"It's so beautiful. So green. Like paradise."

"It is one of the prettiest spots in Ireland," Will admitted. "But there must be some beautiful sights to see where you live."

"Chicago is all glass and steel and concrete. We have a big lake, but it's cold and gray."

Will grabbed her hand. "Come on. Let's go get some lunch. There's a nice restaurant in Killarney I want to take you to. We'll buy you some proper souvenirs and maybe a silly T-shirt with a leprechaun on it."

He took her hand and led her back to where the car was parked. They'd spent most of the morning taking in the beauty of the park with its two beautiful lakes and its sweeping panoramas. Claire wished she'd brought a camera. It would be a perfect scene to paint, the greens and blues and grays.

She sank back into the leather seat of the Mercedes, then reached across the console to take Will's hand. He wove his fingers through hers, then pulled her hand to his lips, pressing a kiss on the back of her wrist. "Are you having a good time?"

"It's wonderful. It's hard to believe that my grandmother grew up here. She seems so at home in Chicago. Why would anyone choose to leave this place?"

"At one time there weren't many jobs here. The country's changed a lot in the last ten years. New businesses have relocated here. And the tourism has increased to be the biggest industry in the country."

"I don't know what it is, but I feel a connection to this place, like it's part of me. Like it's in my blood."

"You are Irish."

"My mother is Norwegian, though," Claire said. "That's where I get the blond hair."

"I like the hair," Will said.

They chatted about the scenery as they drove into Killarney. Claire had seen a bit of the city after their breakfast there. Will had told her it was known primarily as a tourist town, but she found it completely charming with its quaint and colorful buildings and its narrow streets—exactly the way she'd imagined Ireland would be. There were so many shops she'd wanted to explore and Will had promised that he'd take her into every one after lunch.

They took a different route into town and Will pulled off onto a wide road, steering the car back into what looked like a business park. There was a security gate with a guard in a booth. As he pulled the car up to the booth, the guard waved him through with a smile.

"Where are we going?"

"I thought you might like to see this," Will said. "This used to be all mine. Mine and three or four very wealthy investors'." He steered around a sweeping curve and slowed the car. An expansive building stood before them.

"This was yours?"

"It still is, maybe just that far corner of that little building over there. I own a fair bit of stock, but I only work here occasionally. The company is one of the largest employers in the area."

"I'm impressed," Claire said with a grin.

"I don't think you are," Will said.

"I am. It's all very…large. But I have a hard time thinking of you here. I've always known you as the guy who runs the inn. That impresses me, too."

"And that is precisely why I brought you here," he said with a smile.

Will turned around and headed back into Killarney. He pulled into a parking spot on a busy street and they walked the two short blocks to a pretty little restaurant. "They have traditional Irish food here," he said. "There's American fast food in this town, but I thought you'd like this much better."

A waitress showed them to a table that overlooked a small courtyard garden. There were pretty iron tables outside, but the weather was too cold to enjoy sitting out there. Claire ordered a pot of tea and when it arrived, Will stood. "I'll be right back," he said.

"Where are you going?" she asked.

"I won't be long. I promise."

Claire watched as he strode through the restaurant. There were more than a few women who glanced his way as he passed and she felt a tiny sliver of jealousy. It was difficult to think of him with anyone else. But if she left, he'd go on with his life. And before long, he'd find someone to replace her.

Claire took a sip of her tea. Would he feel the same passion and desire he felt for her? Would they share his bed at the inn and would he bring her to the manor house and make love to her in front of the fire?

She shook her head, trying to push the thoughts from her head. The waitress brought a menu and Claire scanned it. In truth, she'd rather go back to Will's house and eat leftovers than sit in this restaurant, unable to touch him or kiss him.

He returned after only ten minutes, rejoining her at the table. "Where did you go?"

He sat down and placed a small box on the table in front of her. "Open it," he said.

"You didn't have to buy me a gift."

"Yes, I did. Go ahead, open it. Don't worry, it's not a sapphire-and-diamond ring."

Claire picked up the box, touched by the gesture. He seemed so pleased with himself that she couldn't help but laugh. "There's not going to be a snake that jumps out, is there?"

"Why would I give you a snake?" Will said. "That's no sort of gift."

"I meant one of those toy snakes, you know, like a gag gift."

He shook his head. "No. There's nothing to fear inside the box. I'm not pulling a prank."

She carefully untied the ribbon and took the lid off the box. Inside was a delicate gold chain with a charm hanging from it. Claire picked it up and held it out in front of her. A red jewel twinkled from the center of the charm. "It's lovely."

"It's a claddagh," Will said.

"I've seen these before, but I don't know what they mean. Is it religious?"

"No," Will said. "More romantic, I should think. There's the heart with the hands on top of it holding a crown. The heart is for love, the hands for friendship and the crown for loyalty." He smiled. "So you can remember me after you go home."

"Did you think I'd forget you?" Claire asked.

He shrugged. "Don't know. I try not to think about it too much."

"It has been wonderful," Claire said, staring down at the claddagh. "I don't think I've ever had a vacation quite like this."

"Exciting?"

"Very exciting. In so many ways."

He reached across the table and took her hand, then began to kiss her fingertips. "You are going back, aren't you?"

Claire nodded. "My life is there, Will. My family and friends. If I stayed here, I wouldn't be able to find work. Irish ad agencies aren't looking for American art directors. But that doesn't mean I won't come back for a visit. Or you could come to Chicago," she suggested.

"I could," he said.

"Will you?"

Will shook his head. "Letting you go once is going to be difficult enough. I don't fancy doing it twice. It's like poking a stick in your eye. The first time might be accidental, but after that, it's just masochistic."

Claire laughed. "It's good we can talk about this," she said. "I don't want my leaving to be sad or full of regrets." She fingered the claddagh, then unhooked the chain and placed it around her neck. "Thank you," she murmured.

Will rose and leaned across the table to kiss her. "You're welcome. Now, let's get out of here. I'm no longer hungry, it seems, and I have the urge to kiss you more thoroughly than this restaurant allows."

He dropped a five-euro note on the table to pay for her tea, then grabbed her hand and pulled her toward the door of the restaurant. When they got outside, they hurried down the street to the car. But at the last second, Will pulled her into a doorway, wrapping his arms around her waist and bringing his mouth down on hers.

He slid his hand beneath her sweater until he cupped her breast in his palm. His broad shoulders hid her from view of anyone passing by, but Claire felt the same tiny thrill of danger that she'd felt that night at the stone circle.

His thumb teased at her nipple and a moan slipped from her throat. "I think I'm through with sightseeing," she murmured.

"There's so much more to see," Will said.

Claire reached down and rubbed her hand over the front of his jeans. "All right, let's do some shopping."

"No, let's go back to my place."

They ran the rest of the way to the car, laughing and grabbing at each other. As they drove out of Killarney, Claire continued to touch him. But Will kept his eyes fixed on the road. When they arrived at his house, they were both nearly out of the car before it came to a stop.

Will fumbled with the keypad to open the front door as Claire tore at his clothes. They both stumbled inside and Will kicked the door shut behind him. "Do you know how happy you make me?" she asked, his lips warm on her neck.

"Deliriously happy?" he returned. "Blissfully happy?"

"Yes," Claire said. "And what makes you happy?"

"Right now? Being here with you. Showing you a bit of Ireland. Thinking about crawling into bed with you."

"So sex makes you happy?"

"Yeah," Will said.

"Funny how that works," Claire said. She slipped out of his arms and raced up the stairs, turning around on the landing to wait for him to catch up. They burst into the bedroom and Will grabbed her by the waist and tossed her onto the bed, then fell down beside her.

"Can we stay here forever?" Claire asked.

"We'll stay for as long as you want," he said.

7

THE LAST CAR FERRY between Fermoy and the Isle of Trall landed at the village at six on Monday evening. Claire stood on the deck and watched as the lights of the town twinkled above the harbor. The captain navigated up to the landing and secured the lines. Then, the winch began to whirl and the ramp was lowered onto dry land.

She glanced over her shoulder to see Will studying her. He sat on the hood of the Mercedes, his foot hitched up on the bumper, his arms braced behind his back. He smiled and a warm feeling rushed through her bloodstream.

Every time he looked at her, she couldn't help but think of the passion they'd shared over the past three days, the way his eyes met hers when he slipped inside of her, the way they remained fixed on hers when he lost himself to his release. Though she'd known him just over a week, it seemed like a lifetime.

They'd grown close so quickly that sometimes it frightened her. And other times, doubts seemed to come at her from all different directions. How much of the attraction was real and how much came from the Druid water she'd given him that night after they'd made love at the stone circle?

She had wanted so desperately to believe that the water had powers, so that it might fix her relationship with Eric. But now, she wanted just the opposite—to know that the water was just water, and the feelings that Will had for her came from his heart and not from some mickey she'd slipped him.

Will motioned her over. Claire pushed away from the rail and joined him at the car. He wrapped his arms around her waist and gave her a kiss. "Are you all right?"

She nodded. "Sure. I'm fine."

"You looked a bit worried."

"No. I'm just hoping that Eric left while we were gone and I won't have to face him again. He would have had to be back for work this morning, so I'm sure he's gone."

Will grabbed her hand and kissed the back of her wrist. "If he's still at the inn, I'll kick him out. He can sleep on the street and take the first ferry out tomorrow morning."

"Thank you. But I know Eric. He'd never think of missing work." In truth, she was more worried about what their return meant to her. As long as they were touring around Ireland, she was still officially on vacation. But now that they were back, Claire had to make a decision about going home herself.

Will helped her into the car and they waited their turn as the four vehicles in front of them drove off. As the last car moved forward, Will maneuvered his car, following the line of taillights into the village.

Eric had offered her a job, a good job, one that she'd be crazy to refuse. But her home was in Chicago and though she might have to live with her grandmother for a while while she found a new apartment, finding another job wouldn't be that difficult. She had plenty of possibilities and lots of connections with other top-notch agencies. What she couldn't do was continue to live at the inn, relying on Will's generosity.

She'd thought about staying. But every ounce of common sense told her that she needed to go home. She'd just broken off a three-year relationship. And Will was her rebound man and rebound relationships never lasted long. And they were from two completely different cultures. That was bound to cause problems at some point. Then there was the fact that everyone she loved would be miles and miles away, so far away that she couldn't get to them quickly.

She'd gone into this relationship with her eyes wide open. It was supposed to be about sex and nothing more. Besides, Will had made no promises, nor asked for any commitments. He knew as well as she did that there would be an end to all of this. Yes, she was being practical. Falling in love with a handsome Irishman who lived on a tiny island had never been part of the plan.

"Thank you for showing me your country," Claire murmured.

"We didn't see much of it beyond the inside of my house." He sent her a sideways glance. "Maybe we can go to Dublin in a few days?"

Claire drew a deep breath, sensing that now would be the best time to broach the subject of her departure. If she waited until they got back to the inn, he would find a way of coaxing her into his bed to delay any conversation at all. Claire had noticed the tactic after Will used it several times over the weekend to great success.

"This was supposed to be a quick trip," she said. "Do you know why I really came to Trall?"

"For the water," Will replied.

Claire gasped. "You knew?"

"It wasn't hard to figure out," he said. "After you told me about Eric, I put two and two together. Plus, some of the folks around town mentioned you were looking for the spring and you tried to get me to tell you where it was."

"The point is I have to go home. I only intended to stay for a few days and it's been a week."

"Why do you have to go?" Will asked.

"Because I don't live here?"

"You don't have a job, you don't have a fiancé. In a month or two, you aren't going to have a place to live. What do you have back there that's so bloody important?"

"A life," Claire said. "This is your life, not mine, Will. I just stumbled into it. And believe me, it's been wonderful. But we can't continue to live like this. Life is not a vacation."

Will didn't say a word as they drove toward the inn. He pulled the car into the drive and parked it in front, then turned off the ignition. "What if I gave you a reason to stay?" he said softly.

She'd gone into her affair with Will knowing there would be an end to it when she went home. No-strings sex was supposed to mean just that—no attachments! Was he looking for some strings now? "I—I'm not sure

I could," Claire said. "I just can't uproot my life and move halfway around the world for—" She swallowed hard.

"For a man you don't love?" Will asked.

"No," Claire replied. "For someone I met a week ago."

He drew a deep breath and nodded. "I understand. There's not much on this island for a girl like yourself."

That wasn't true, Claire thought. There were a few things she'd never found anywhere else—a man who made her feel beautiful and sexy and exciting, for one. There was a big, Elizabethan bed that made her feel warm and safe. There was a community of charming and outrageous people who had accepted her as if she'd lived on Trall her entire life.

But she'd spent three years with Eric, believing what they had was a future—and she'd been wrong. How could she possibly make the decision to stay with Will after just one week? Her feelings had nothing to do with love. It was lust and she ought to be willing to admit that and move on.

"You don't have to stay forever," he said softly. "Just stay for one more week. And at the end of that week, you can decide whether you want to stay for another. It's that simple, Claire."

"I'll have to think about it," she replied, forcing a smile. Claire opened the car door and stepped out, knowing that she was just a word or two from being convinced the other way. She just needed the right reason to overwhelm all the purely practical reasons she'd listed in her head.

Will grabbed their bags from the backseat and caught

up with her at the front door. "Promise me you will consider it," he said.

"I promise."

When they stepped inside, the inn was quiet. Will dropped the bags at the door, then helped Claire out of her jacket. They walked toward the parlor, drawn by the fire in the hearth. But just as they entered the room, Sorcha's head popped up from the sofa.

"You're home," she said, running her hands through her tousled hair.

"You're here," Will replied.

An instant later, Eric sat up beside Sorcha, a sheepish grin on his face. His hair was also mussed, a clear indication of what they'd been doing together on the sofa. Claire glanced at Will and he wrinkled his nose.

She turned her attention back to Eric, who was now fumbling with the buttons of his shirt. "I thought you'd be gone," she said.

"I like it here," Eric replied, grinning at Sorcha. "I thought I needed a break."

Claire cleared her throat, stunned by the scene playing out in front of her. "But—but don't you have a new job you need to get back to?"

He shook his head. "I've always been way too obsessed with work. And for that, I'd like to apologize, Claire. I know it must have been difficult for you, living with me. But back then, I just didn't have my priorities straight."

"Back then?" Claire asked. "Eric, that was a week ago. You came here three days ago determined to talk me into returning with you. And now suddenly, you're not interested in going home?"

"There's more to life than work, right, Will?"

Will nodded reluctantly. "I've always believed that."

"Stop," Claire said. "Eric, this is not you. You can't walk away from this job. I don't know what's been going on here, but you need to get back to New York. Now."

"Sorcha thinks I should stay," he said.

"I do," Sorcha added. "He seems to like it here. And he has all sorts of ideas about how we could increase tourism on the island."

Claire groaned, pressing her fingertips to her temples, as she turned back to Eric. "You've been listening to Sorcha? Has she given you anything to eat or drink? You do realize that she's a sorceress, Eric." Sorcha had cast some kind of spell on Eric or fed him a potion. It was the only explanation for his behavior. Claire calmed herself. "Sorcha knows nothing about the advertising world, how competitive it is, how important it is to make the right career moves. Don't mess this up, Eric. You'll regret it forever."

"Relax," Eric said, flopping back on the sofa.

"No, I'm not going to relax. You're going home, tomorrow. On the first flight we can get out of here. Where is your ticket? I'm going to call the airline right now."

"But I like it here," Eric insisted. He grabbed Sorcha by the waist and pulled her down on top of him. "The people are really friendly."

Claire screamed in frustration. "You only like it here because you're not thinking clearly. This is an island, Eric, without a health club or a Starbucks or place to buy expensive Italian shoes. You wouldn't survive a week here."

"I've changed."

Claire looked at Sorcha. "What have you done to him?"

"Don't look at me," Sorcha said.

"You're the one who put a spell on him."

"Only because Will asked me to," she said.

"I did not!" Will cried. He looked at Claire. "I didn't, I swear. I asked her to keep him occupied. There's a big difference between taking him on a tour of the island and snogging him on my sofa."

"Why would you tell her to do that?"

"So I could spend time with you!"

Eric held up his hand, then sat up. "Wait a second. You two are…"

"Nothing," Claire snapped. "It's none of your business what we are. Now, which room are you in?" She turned to Will. "Which room is he in?"

"Six," Will said.

Claire strode to the desk in the entry hall and grabbed the spare key from the board. "I'm going upstairs to get him packed and then I'm going to try to see if I can get us *both* a flight home."

With that, Claire turned and walked toward the stairs. By the time she reached the top, she knew she'd made the right decision. She'd go to New York with Eric, she'd take the job at his agency and she'd start her life all over again. And in a few months' time, her vacation in Ireland, and her affair with Will Donovan, would be nothing more than a pleasant memory.

She found Eric's room and opened the door, then stood and stared at the rumpled sheets on the bed. Sorcha's bra hung from the bedpost. Claire ought to have been angry or jealous or felt some emotion. The man she'd slept with up until a week ago had been bedding another woman. And yet, she felt absolutely nothing—beyond mild irritation.

With a soft curse, she walked into the room and grabbed his overnight bag, then began to gather his things.

"What are you doing?"

Claire closed her eyes at the sound of Will's voice. "I'm getting him packed. He's going home. I should have never gone with you. I should have made sure he went back to New York instead of running away from my problems."

"That's not fair," Will said. "You can't blame this on yourself."

"Who should I blame it on—you?"

Will cursed beneath his breath. "He's a grown man. He can damn well do as he pleases!"

"He's going home," Claire said. "He won't last a week on this island. And once he realizes what he's given up, he'll blame me."

"And you're going with him?"

"I'm afraid that's the only way to get him on the plane," Claire said. She tossed a folded shirt into the bag, then faced Will. "What were you thinking setting Sorcha on him?"

"I told you, I needed him distracted."

"Seduced was more like it," Claire muttered, snatching Sorcha's bra from the bedpost and throwing it at him.

"So what?" Will said as he tossed the bra onto the bed. "What is so bloody wrong with that? I wanted you to myself for a few days. I thought Sorcha was the best way to accomplish that. I know what I have to offer here isn't what you want, Claire. I could promise to make it more, but I'm not sure that it would change your mind. Jaysus, I used to have everything a woman could possibly want, but I didn't want any of the women who wanted it. Now, I have nothing that you want, but I want you."

"It wasn't supposed to last," Claire cried. "We agreed on that, don't you remember?"

"Well, forgive me," Will said softly. "I needed to make this last as long as I could, so I called on Sorcha. How do you Americans say it? I gave it my best shot? I put all my cards on the table?"

"Maybe it's better this way," she muttered. "As long as I didn't have a good reason to leave, I might never have gone. But I'm not going to be responsible for Eric screwing up his professional life because of that...witch."

"And what about all the good reasons *you* have to stay?" Will asked.

"Those are the same reasons that will make me come back," Claire said, turning to him. "This doesn't have to mean it's over between us. We could see each other again."

"Right," Will said, nodding.

She found Eric's ticket in the breast pocket of his jacket and handed it to Will. "My ticket is on the mantel in my room. We're both flying the same airline. Could you call and see if they can get us out on a flight early tomorrow morning?"

"Are you going to New York with Eric or home to Chicago?" Will asked.

Claire thought about her answer for a long moment. "New York," she said. "Actually, the flight goes in and out of Newark, so just tell them I'm getting off there."

Will plucked the ticket from her fingers and turned for the door. He closed it behind him without saying another word. Claire tipped her head back and sighed. Now all she needed to do was convince herself that she'd made the right decision.

WILL POURED A GLASS of whiskey, then leaned forward and braced his forearms on the worktable. The day he'd been dreading was coming and there was nothing he could do about it. He'd done as she'd asked and called the airline. Claire and Eric were scheduled on a flight out of Shannon at 10:00 a.m. tomorrow morning. They'd have to leave on the first ferry at daybreak to get to the mainland in time. He had less than twelve hours left with her.

He took a swig of the whiskey, the drink burning his throat as it went down. "Not enough time," he murmured.

Claire would be leaving tomorrow and he'd be left to go back to the life he'd enjoyed before she'd arrived on his doorstep. He thought back to that night, a week ago, when she'd stood in the entry hall, dripping water all over the parquet floor. From the moment he first set eyes on her, there'd been an undeniable attraction. He'd done nothing to resist and now, he'd pay the price.

"Can I have some?"

Will glanced up to find Sorcha standing in the doorway. He slid the bottle in her direction. "Help yourself."

She grabbed a glass from the cabinet and dumped whiskey into it. "I'm sorry. I just couldn't resist."

"I'm not angry," Will said. "You have your needs and who am I to keep you from satisfying them?"

"He's kind of dishy," Sorcha said. "And he has an incredible body and he's smart and funny. And he thinks I'm interesting and mysterious and clever."

Will stood, then leaned back against the counter, his hands braced on the edge. "Please, tell me you haven't been to bed with him."

"All right, I haven't been to bed with him. Does that make you feel better?"

Will groaned. "No, because you're lying."

"I'm a big girl, Will. I do as I please. Without encouragement from you. And you had your time with your American, so what are you so angry about?"

"I'm not angry," he said.

Sorcha stared him for a long moment, then groaned. "Oh, bloody hell. You've gone and fallen in love with her, haven't you?"

"And what if I have?"

"Did you learn nothing from me, Will? Sex is a wonderful thing, and it's even more wonderful when it's good sex. But good sex does not mean you have to monogram the bed linens and look for a good buy on a set of china. It's just sex, that's all."

"You don't know that."

"She lives across an ocean," Sorcha said. "Have I said enough?" She held up her hand. "And don't tell me love can conquer all, because that's just sentimental shite."

"I used to appreciate your cynicism, but it's wearing on me."

Sorcha raked her hair out of her eyes and studied him intently. "You really love her, then? You're not just confusing lust with love?"

Will shook his head. "Nope. I think I really love her."

"Then you should tell her."

He couldn't deny he'd been thinking about doing just that all weekend. He'd come close Saturday night, when he'd tricked her into saying it. In truth, he'd hoped she might tell him that she loved him for more than one night—but she hadn't. "Do you know how ridiculous that would sound? I've known her for a week. You can't just fall in love in a week."

"Of course you can," Sorcha said. "It's called love at first sight. People do it all the time. What you're saying is that *you* can't fall in love in one week."

"If she wanted to stay, she'd stay. I've already asked her, more than once. But you'll notice she jumped at the first chance to go home with her ex-fiancé."

"They were never engaged," Sorcha said.

"I think I have my answer right there. Hell, she even asked me to make the flight arrangements."

"Then why don't you go live with her? You've been to the States before and you've told me how much you like it."

"I haven't been invited," he said.

Sorcha pressed her hands flat on the worktable and leaned toward him. "God's teeth, you are the thickest git I've ever known. If you want the woman, then grab her. Don't think about it, just do it."

"If we're supposed to be together, then it will happen. But I don't think we'll know for sure until we spend some time apart."

"Fine. Muck up your life if you want. But don't come bawling to me when you're all sad and lonely. I'm not going to give you a bit of sympathy." Sorcha gulped down the last of her whiskey, then smoothed her hands over her rumpled dress. "If you'll excuse me, I'm taking Eric to the pub so that we might spend our last night together in a more jolly atmosphere. You should use the opportunity to enjoy yourself."

Will gave Sorcha a weak wave as she left the kitchen. Then he poured himself another whiskey and drank it down in one gulp, the liquid warming his stomach. He heard the front door slam and he picked up his glass and set it in the sink, then headed back out to the parlor. Will walked to the fireplace and tossed more peat onto the fire. He stepped back and watched as the flames licked at the fresh fuel.

Had Sorcha told him his life would turn around completely in a week, Will might have called her daft. But it was as if she had known something momentous was going to happen that night when Claire arrived. Perhaps he knew it, too.

He'd been waiting for the right moment to move forward and the moment was here. He could either choose to ignore it and wait for the next moment, or he could take one more chance with Claire and see where it led.

Will turned and walked up the stairs. Eric's room was empty, his bags packed and sitting next to the bed. He continued down the hall to Claire's room and he found her, sitting on the edge of the bed, setting her travel alarm. "Your flight is at ten tomorrow morning," he said. "You'll have to catch the six a.m. ferry. The mail boat doesn't leave until noon. I'll call a car to pick you up in Fermoy and take you to the airport."

"Sorcha said she would drive us," Claire replied. "Did you tell Eric?"

Will shook his head. "I told Sorcha. She and Eric went into town for some supper. I could make something for us both if you're hungry."

"No. We had a late lunch. I just need a good night's sleep," she said with an apologetic smile. "We didn't get much sleep this weekend, did we?"

The meaning of her words was clear. They wouldn't spend the night together. In truth, it was better that way. He'd never be able to watch her leave after spending the night in her bed. It was better to make the break now, before they got caught up in something more.

"Well, if you want something to eat later, the kitchen is always open."

"Thanks."

Will shoved his hands in his back pockets, unsure of what to say next. Was he supposed to pour out his heart to her, to tell her he couldn't live without her? Should he beg her to stay? Or should they make plans to see each other again? He cleared his throat and smiled tightly. "I suppose we ought to say our goodbyes now." He watched as she reached up and fingered the claddagh, as if it were some charm to help her maintain her resolve.

"All right. Well, then." She stepped forward and held out her arms.

Will reluctantly took her into his embrace, burying his face in the curve of her neck and inhaling her sweet scent. He closed his eyes, memorizing the feel of her body against his, enjoying the warmth. He would miss her, but maybe there would come a day when he wouldn't think about the time they spent together, when an image of her wouldn't drift through his head every few minutes.

He stepped back and then placed a gentle kiss on her lips. "You take care, Claire," he said.

"You, too," she said. "And if you're ever in New York, look me up."

It took all his willpower to let her go, to pull his hands from her body and place them back at his sides. He took a deep breath and walked to the door, then forced himself to walk through without looking back. When Will got downstairs, he grabbed his keys from the front table in the entry hall and walked out into the chilly night.

A soft rain had begun to fall and Will turned his face up to the sky. He would get through this. It felt like a loss because he'd grown so accustomed to having her around. But once she was gone, he'd make a point to get off the island more, to meet and date new women.

Will walked to his car and got inside, then steered out of the drive. When he turned onto the road into the village, he went in the opposite direction. Reaching for the radio, he cranked the sound up until the booming bass of a U2 song filled the inside of the Mercedes. The wipers kept an uneven rhythm as rain pelted against the windscreen.

He reached the road that led to the stone circle and Will took it, bumping over the rough, rutted surface and skidding in the mud. When he reached the end, he stopped the car and stared into the darkness, the landscape illuminated only by the headlamps.

Restless, Will got out, leaving the engine running and the headlamps on. The wind-driven rain now lashed at his skin, like cold shards of glass striking his face. Will walked toward the stone circle, the path imprinted on his brain from his teenage years.

The stone pillars loomed in the darkness and Will walked to the center and lay down on the stone altar. He stared up at the sky, black and moonless. In the distance he could hear the ocean crashing against the cliffs. Without a jacket, the rain had soaked his shirt and jeans. But the cold seemed to numb him to everything he was feeling.

Will closed his eyes and waited for the rain to wash her from his thoughts. But nothing he did could rid himself of the memories—the feel of her skin and the scent of her hair, the sound of her voice and the sight of her naked body. She'd found a way into his heart and Will knew he would be less of a man when she was gone.

He was in love with Claire and there was nothing he could do for it.

THE LIGHTS ON the ground floor of the inn were still ablaze when Will returned hours later. He wasn't even sure what time it was, only that it was well past midnight. He'd stayed out at the stone circle until the cold was too much to bear.

His clothes were soaked and drops of water clung to his hair. He'd thought about staying out all night and only returning to the inn after he was sure she was gone. It would be impossible to sleep with her just one floor above him. But there was a half bottle of whiskey waiting in the kitchen. If that didn't put him to sleep, at least it would dull the need to see her just once more before she left.

He kicked off his shoes and walked through the dining room into the kitchen. Will didn't bother with the glass and, instead, grabbed the bottle and took a long swallow. The whiskey warmed his belly and slowly began to ease the chill in his limbs.

But it did nothing to erase the thoughts of Claire from his head. Without thinking, he walked back to the entry hall, then climbed the stairs. When he reached her room, Will tested the door and found it unlocked. He didn't hesitate, just walked inside.

The bathroom light was on, illuminating the room enough to make out the details of Claire's face. She was asleep, her hands folded in front of her, her hair tumbled over her eyes. Will squatted down next to the bed and drank in the sight of her.

But it was like she was untouchable, like she was already gone, the distance between them growing with every second that passed. He set the whiskey bottle on the bedside table, then reached out and gently brushed the hair out of her eyes. But it wasn't enough to just look at her. He leaned over and pressed his lips to her forehead, lingering there as he inhaled the scent of her hair.

When he drew back, her eyes were open. They stared at each other for a long time, neither one of them moving or speaking. Then Claire pushed up on her elbow and touched her lips to his, her hand slipping around his neck to draw him near. When she pulled back, her fingers skimmed over his wet clothes and she frowned.

Claire sat up and swung her legs off the side of the bed. She began to work at the buttons of his shirt, the damp fabric making it more difficult. Will's teeth chattered, but he wasn't sure if it was from the cold or from the excitement of being with her again.

He watched her as she slowly undressed him, his arms at his sides. Will was almost afraid to touch her, afraid that she might change her mind and ask him to leave. When she'd stripped off all of his clothes, she crawled back into bed, holding the covers up in a silent invitation.

He settled in beside her and she pulled off the nightgown she was wearing and tossed it on the floor. The bed was warm from the heat of her body and they lay facing each other, their foreheads pressed together. Claire slowly rubbed his arm, then his back, then reached out and drew him against her body.

A sigh slipped from his throat as Will began to feel the numbness subside, replaced by delicious warmth, which coursed through his body with every heartbeat. They began to touch each other, tentatively at first. But it didn't take long for desire to overcome them both.

Will captured her mouth in a kiss filled with a bitter-sweet need. He wouldn't ask for anything more than just this one last night together.

He pulled her beneath him, his hips nestled between her legs. Will reached down and drew her knees up and he began to rock against her. Her body was soft and pliant and so warm. The feel of her naked skin against his own was almost more than he could handle.

Though he wanted to bury himself inside her, Will was acutely aware that he didn't have a condom. Finding one would require leaving her room and there was no telling what might happen if he did. So instead, he decided to find his release—and hers—in other ways.

He moved against her, the base of his shaft sliding along the moist slit between her legs. She moaned softly and arched toward him, her breath coming in tiny gasps. Their rhythm became steady and Will closed his eyes, enjoying the friction between them.

And then suddenly, Claire pulled away and when they met again and he moved, he slipped inside of her. Will froze, surprised at the mistake. She was warm and wet and ready and it had happened so quickly. But as Claire began to move again, Will realized that it hadn't been a mistake. She knew exactly what she was doing and she wanted him this way.

Will groaned as wild sensations raced through his body. There was nothing between them now. The last barrier had fallen and they were completely vulnerable to each other. Her warmth surrounded him, enveloped him, caressed him, and he felt himself grow harder with each stroke.

Claire began to moan softly, tiny sounds escaping her throat with each thrust. And when she shifted beneath him, Will sensed she was close. He pulled out and rubbed up against her for a time, then slipped back inside.

Her breath came in soft gasps and he continued like that until she was clutching at his shoulders and delirious with desire. Only then did he allow himself to surrender to the incredible pleasure that he felt.

Slowly, they climbed together, their movements now frantic, Claire arching against him with every thrust. Will felt her tighten around him and then she dissolved into a series of powerful spasms, her breath catching her throat with each one. He drove into her one last time and then let himself go, his orgasm exploding deep inside of her.

They continued to move together, still consumed with pleasure, as they came back down from the heights. Will knew he could go all night. He'd never have enough of her. But what they had shared had been absolutely perfect and he wouldn't spoil it.

He lay down next to her and pulled her body against his, tucking her backside into his lap and resting his chin on her shoulder. Claire grabbed his hands and clasped them in front of her, pressing her lips to each palm.

She fell asleep that way, nestled against him. Will listened to her breathing grow soft and slow. He closed his eyes and tried to join her, but his thoughts kept him from relaxing. He'd been living in a fantasy this past week and had made a conscious effort not to think about the future. But now, it was *all* he could think about.

Where was he supposed to go from here? Would he

ever be able to feel the same kind of passion for another woman as he felt for Claire? He had to find answers for his questions or they would drive him right 'round the bend.

He didn't sleep. He lay in her bed until the first hints of day began to brighten the sky. The clock on the beside table ticked down their last minutes together and when it read 5:00 a.m., Will knew it was time to leave. Sorcha would pick them up in less than an hour and he didn't plan to be around when they left.

Will kissed Claire's shoulder, then gently slipped from beneath the covers. He collected his clothes, tugging on his damp jeans but tucking the rest beneath his arm. He gave her one last look, satisfied he was ready to walk away. And then, he opened the door and stepped out into the hall.

His footsteps were silent against the thick oriental carpet on the stairs. Will walked back to his room and exchanged his jeans for a pair of fleece sweatpants. He pulled a hooded sweatshirt over his head and then slipped into a clean pair of socks and his trainers. As he walked out the kitchen door, Will remembered that he hadn't tallied the charges for either Claire or Eric.

He didn't care. The cost of having them stay at the inn was far greater than anything he could charge. He couldn't buy his heart back with the money, nor could he soothe his soul, so he didn't want it.

Pulling the hood up over his head, Will squinted into the predawn darkness, waiting for his eyes to adjust. And then he began to run. The cold air cleared his head and filled his lungs as his feet pounded against the road.

His breath clouded in front of his face. One step after another, he ran, as if he could drive the last memory of her out of his body.

He jogged along the waterfront, then wove his way back through town, past the bakery and tea shop. The scent of freshly baked bread drifted through the air and Will slowed, then stopped and walked back to the bakery. He might as well get back to his regular routine as quickly as possible.

Mary Kearney smiled at him as he walked inside. "'Tis himself, out for his morning run. I haven't seen ye in a week's time," she said. "I hear you've been keepin' yourself busy with that pretty American girl."

"Not anymore," Will said. "She's on her way back home this morning."

Mary put two raisin scones in a paper bag, then retrieved a bottle of apple juice from the refrigerated case behind the counter. "I'll put it on your tab," she said.

Will took his breakfast and continued his jog, out of town and up the long rise above the harbor. He had a favorite spot where he usually sat in the early morning, a place where he watched the ferry and fishing boats move in and out of the harbor at daybreak.

The sky was just beginning to turn pink in the east when he saw the cars begin to line up at the ferry landing. There were a number of people who worked on the mainland every day. Occasionally, the ferry was booked for its maximum load of eight cars. But Sorcha would have called to reserve a spot.

Will opened the bag and grabbed one of the scones, still warm from the oven. He took a bite and waited, watching for the little red Volvo that Sorcha drove. When he saw it, he felt his heart twist in his chest, knowing that Claire was inside.

A few minutes later, the ferry moved out into the waters of the small bay, Sorcha's red car onboard. He was too far away to see the faces of the people on deck, but Will thought he recognized Claire's jacket.

He smiled to himself. She was thinking of him. He could feel it, could sense it across the distance between them. She was wondering if she'd made a mistake in leaving, wondering why he hadn't been there to say goodbye, wondering if they'd ever see each other again.

"Goodbye, Claire," he murmured. "Have a good life."

He tossed the remains of the scone into the tall grass, then began his jog back into town. Katie could take care of the inn. He hadn't even unpacked from his last trip off the island. He could grab his bags and catch the next ferry.

He couldn't stay here. And he couldn't go back to the country house. All he knew was that he had to find a place that didn't remind him of Claire. And after he did that, maybe he'd be able to imagine a future without her.

8

CLAIRE RECHECKED her ticket and then looked at the departure time posted above the desk. Eric sat next to her, his arms crossed over his chest, his expression glum.

"You look like I just ran over your dog," Claire said.

He scowled. "You didn't have to drag me out of there like some bratty kid. I was planning to leave on my own."

"Oh, I don't think so. You don't know the power Sorcha Mulroony has over men."

"Right," he said. "So she's hot in the sack. There's reason enough to stay in Ireland."

"I don't want to hear this," Claire said, covering her ears with her hands. "Even though we aren't together anymore, it's only been a week. It's just not right to be throwing that in my face."

"Sorry," Eric muttered. "But what about you? You weren't exactly pining away for me. You ran off with Will."

"I'll admit, maybe you and I didn't belong together. And maybe you were right to break up with me. You saved us both a lot of future heartache—or at least me."

"Me, too," Eric said. "I never wanted to hurt you, Claire. Things just started getting so crazy and I didn't know how to handle it. The more I thought about getting married, the more I felt my life spinning out of control. I just needed some time to think. I handled it badly and I'm sorry."

"You've been saying that a lot lately. I guess I almost believe you."

"So, do you believe me enough to take the job in New York?" Eric asked. "I know you'd be great at it. And we'd make a good team."

The offer was tempting. It would solve almost all her problems. She'd get a great salary, live in a wonderful city and be so busy that she'd forget all about Will Donovan in short order. "I'm thinking about it. I'd like to see the offices, maybe spend some time in New York, meet some of the people at the agency."

Eric grinned and Claire had a difficult time staying mad at him. They might end up being good friends. It would be nice to have a friend in New York.

"I'm going to get something to drink." Eric rose from his seat. "They're not going to call us for another ten or fifteen minutes. Do you want anything?"

Claire shook her head. "I'll be fine." She watched as Eric left the gate area and walked out to the concourse. How could her feelings have changed so quickly? She looked at him now and saw a guy who was flawed and fallible, not the Prince Charming she'd always dreamed of. But he wasn't a bad guy, just not *her* guy.

If it hadn't been for Eric, she never would have met Will. One good thing came from the three years she'd spent with him. She'd found herself in Ireland. She'd left behind the measured, orderly person she'd been in

Chicago and discovered a wildly passionate, spontaneous woman who was better suited to a life led by her heart than by her head.

"Is it almost time to board?"

Claire glanced up to find Sorcha standing in front of her. Sorcha had dropped them off nearly an hour ago, taking her time to give Eric an unforgettable kiss. "What are you doing back here?"

Sorcha waved a ticket beneath Claire's nose. "Eric invited me to New York and I've decided to go. I've always wanted to see New York. I've heard it's a wonderful place."

"But what about your shop?" Claire asked. "I thought Trall was your home."

"You can't have an adventure staying home," she said. "And life should be a big adventure, don't you think?"

"Are you sure you know what you're doing?"

Sorcha hesitated, a frown furrowing her brow. "Oh, no. I haven't interfered in a reconciliation, have I?"

"No," Claire replied. "No, Eric and I will not be getting back together."

"Well, good. Then you and Will have a chance. He loves you to bits, you know. I'm not sure he'll ever be able to live without you."

Claire smiled. "Don't be silly, we've never—"

"He told me he loved you," Sorcha said. "Of course, he couldn't say it to you. Men can be so thickheaded sometimes. When really they're just big old babies."

"He really said he loves me?"

"The thing is, he gave you some of the Druid water, so he thinks that's why things were so…

powerful between you two." She frowned. "He's never believed in the magic before. Odd time to start, don't you think?"

"I gave him some of the Druid water, too," Claire said. "That makes us even."

Sorcha grabbed Claire's hands as she sat down beside her. "I'm going to be honest with you. And this is coming from a Druid sorceress. I don't know that the water is anything but water. Personally, I think it's probably all just crap. But though it may have given you a push in the right direction, there's more to you and Will than the water has made."

If Sorcha, a certified Druid, didn't believe in the power of the water, then Claire would seriously have to reconsider her opinion in the matter. "I don't know what to do," she murmured.

Sorcha reached into her purse and withdrew her car keys. "I'll make sure Eric gets back to New York. You go back to Trall and continue what you started with Will. You can take my car…you can stay in my flat above the shop. It would be nice if you opened the shop every now and again. And if you need to mix a potion, all my recipes are in a notebook under the cash drawer. The key is on the ring."

Claire tried to think of all the reasons that she shouldn't go back. But she wasn't that person anymore, the girl who carefully thought out every single decision, who made lists of the pros and cons, who tried to weigh every move against her future happiness. At this very moment, she was thinking with her heart—and her heart told her to follow Sorcha's advice.

Claire snatched the keys from her fingers, then threw her arms around Sorcha's neck. "Thank you," she said. "I promise I'll take good care of the shop. When are you coming back?"

"I don't know," Sorcha said. "I'm not going to think about the future."

Claire grabbed up her bag and slipped it onto her shoulder. "You'll explain to Eric. And you promise you'll make him go back to work tomorrow?"

"I promise," Sorcha replied. "The car is in G-9, to the right when you get out of the elevator. Oh, and you'll have to stop for petrol. It's almost empty."

Claire gave Sorcha another hug, then hurried down the concourse. She wouldn't be able to retrieve her checked luggage, but she could afford to wait a day or two for that. She'd probably have to go to the airlines and inform them of her change in plans. But she could be back on the island by late afternoon.

"Hey, where are you going?"

Claire stopped, then turned around. Eric had passed her by. "I'm going back to Trall. Sorcha is waiting for you at the gate. She's going to New York with you."

Eric's eyes lit up. "Oh, yeah?"

"Go to work tomorrow. I'm going to call and see if you're there."

"What about the job?" he asked.

Claire shrugged. "I think I'm going to have to turn you down. Sorry!" She gave him an apologetic smile, waved and then headed down the concourse. As she walked, Claire felt an amazing sense of anticipation. Sorcha had been right. Life was an adventure. She had no idea how Will would react when she returned to the island. But if Sorcha had been telling the truth, then he'd be happy to see her.

By the time she left the airport it was nearly noon. The flight had been delayed and she was able to get her luggage back. The car had been more difficult. She'd searched the car park for nearly an hour before she found it, parked in B-5 rather than G-9. A friendly security guard had driven her around the lot until she spotted the red Volvo with the Druids Unite! bumper sticker.

Claire tossed her bags in the backseat, started up the car and drove out of the lot. Navigating was tricky. Reading the map and driving at the same time took careful coordination, but within a few minutes she was headed away from the airport and into Limerick. She carefully followed the signs for Tralee, knowing that they would put her on the right highway.

But as she came closer and closer to the city, Claire began to doubt her decision to return. If she went back to Trall, then she was making a commitment to a future with Will. It was a huge decision. Maybe she ought to take a bit more time to make sure she was ready. Was Will really in love with her or was that just some sort of fantasy that Sorcha had cooked up? Was she in love with him or was she caught up in the romance of it all? Going back only to find out there was nothing there in the first place would be horrible.

On her way toward Tralee, Claire saw a sign for Castlemaine and remembered their time at Will's country house. Something had happened there. They'd imagined themselves in love, but perhaps it had been more real than either of them had known.

By the time Claire reached the ferry landing, she was filled with a mixture of emotions. She wanted to see Will again, but she was afraid. She wanted to tell him how she felt, but she wasn't sure her feelings would be reciprocated. And she wanted to begin her new life in Ireland, but without Will, that would never happen.

The moment she drove the car onto the ferry, she would be making a leap of faith. And though none of this was planned or considered carefully or put on one of her lists, this felt right. And if she'd learned nothing else in Ireland, she'd learned to listen to her heart and not her head.

WILL STARED at his laptop screen, the lines of code blurring in front of his eyes. He reached for his mug of coffee and took a sip, only to find it cold. Glancing around the Internet café, he searched for a waitress but they had all disappeared. The Dublin lunch crowd had thinned and there were just a few students sitting at the tables now.

He got up and strolled to the counter and set his mug down, and the young man working the espresso machine promptly refilled it. Will had come to Dublin for lack of a better place to go. He'd thought about Switzerland or Italy, but in the end had come to Dublin to see his family. Time spent with his two nieces and his nephew was enough to distract himself from thoughts of Claire.

It had been nearly a week and he'd checked his

messages on his mobile and his e-mail, hoping that she'd at least write to tell him that she'd arrived safely in New York. But there'd been nothing, no word, no indication that she was even thinking about him.

He knew he'd have to return to Trall before long. But Will kept hoping he'd wake up one day and manage at least an hour without thinking about her. Perhaps it was time to go out and find another career for himself. He'd never intended to run the inn forever. His career in hospitality had been just a stopgap, something to do while he figured out the rest of his life.

It was time to move on, he thought to himself. His sister and her husband had talked about moving back to the island from Dublin. And if they did, then his parents would probably follow and the inn would be in good hands.

Will's mobile rang and he pulled it out of his jacket pocket and checked the identification. Each time it rang, he couldn't help but hope it was Claire on the other end. When he saw International Call on the screen, Will's heart stopped. Was this finally her?

Will flipped open the phone. "Hello?"

"Hello, Will Donovan! Do you know who this is?"

He recognized Sorcha's voice. "Hello, Sorcha." He hadn't talked to Sorcha since Eric and Claire had left. He'd taken the afternoon ferry, before she would have been back from the airport. "Where are you calling from?"

"Where do you think? The Big Apple. But for the life of me, I can't understand why it's called that. There aren't any orchards here. And I haven't seen a single statue commemorating fruit."

"You're in New York?" Will asked. "What are you doing there?"

"I came with Eric. Last week. Didn't Claire tell you?"

"I haven't talked to Claire since she left."

"Well, isn't it a bit hard to avoid her?"

"Sorcha, what the hell are you talking about?"

"Where are you?"

"I'm in Dublin, visiting my family. I left right after you did."

There was nothing but silence on the other end of the phone. "Will, I think you'd better go home. Claire didn't come to New York with us. She went back to the island. I gave her my car and the keys to my flat. If you don't get back there soon, she might just leave again."

"Why the hell didn't you call me?" Will said as he gathered up his things.

"I thought you knew. I assumed that she would have gone directly to the inn to speak to you."

"You're saying she's on Trall," Will murmured.

"Do we have a bad connection?" Sorcha asked. "Yes, she's on Trall. And I've been trying to get hold of her, but she doesn't return my calls. I don't think she knows how to work my answering machine. So, when you get back, I need you to tell her about the fuse box. If she uses the toaster and the microwave at the same time, the fuse blows. And I want her to call me and tell me how things are going at the shop. There's a shipment of beads coming in next week and I want to make sure she knows how to pay for them."

"Are you sure she's in Ireland?"

"Well, she's not in New York. I suppose she could have gone back to Chicago."

"I have to go," Will said.

"You'll tell her?"

"Yes, if she's on Trall, I'll give her the message. Give me your number. I'll call you back as soon as I talk to her."

He scribbled down the number, then said goodbye to Sorcha. Will snapped the phone shut and closed his eyes, taking a moment to digest everything that Sorcha had told him. Claire hadn't gotten on the plane, she wasn't in New York and there was a good chance she was waiting for him on Trall.

Will hit the memory dial for the inn and glanced at his watch. If there were no guests, then Katie wouldn't be there. He let the phone ring for thirty seconds, then hung up. If Claire was back on the island, then someone would have to know. Annie Mulroony? Dennis Fraser? He decided to call Mary Kearney, only because he had her number programmed into his phone.

She picked up after two rings. "Mary, this is Will Donovan."

"Hello, Will. How is Dublin?"

Will didn't bother to ask how she knew he was in Dublin. Obviously Katie had mentioned it to someone on the island and word had gotten round. "Dublin is fine. Mary, have you seen Claire O'Connor around?"

"Sure. I just saw her this morning. She came in for scones and a cup of coffee. Ye picked a fine time to leave the island."

"I realize that," Will said. "If you see her again, would you let her know that I'm on my way back?"

"I will, ye can be sure of that," Mary said.

Will said his goodbye, then grabbed up his things from the café. He could go back to his parents' house to pick up his bags, but that would waste at least an hour. It would take him at least four hours to get back to Fermoy and then nearly an hour on the ferry, if he got to the ferry in time. He could always hire a helicopter. But he needed time to think before he saw her again. The drive would provide that time.

Will stood up, then drew a deep breath. This was good news. This was great news! For whatever reason, Claire couldn't leave. She'd come back to Trall for a reason and he had to believe that she'd returned for him—for them.

Will had made the drive between the ferry landing and Dublin too many times to count. It had always been a pleasant drive and he'd never felt the need to rush. But as he steered the car through the busy streets of Dublin, he was impatient to reach his destination.

He put a CD into the player and tried to calm his thoughts. He let his mind spin back to the first time he'd seen Claire. The attraction had been instant. What was it about her that he'd found so fascinating? Was it the vulnerability? Or was it her strength? She was such a mass of contradictions that he never knew how she'd react. On the surface, she seemed prim and proper, but underneath, she was also a tease and a temptress. She could be serious and silly and stubborn and spontaneous. Life would never be dull living with Claire.

It was dark by the time he got to Fermoy. He arrived with just ten minutes to spare and drove right onto the ferry. He recognized everyone on board and found it odd after being virtually anonymous in Dublin. Still, it felt good to be going home—and better yet, to be going home to Claire.

He walked over to the wheelhouse of the ferry and waved at Eddie Donahue. "Did you take Claire O'Connor over to Trall earlier this week?"

Eddie thought about it for a moment, then nodded. "Pretty blonde, American, driving Sorcha Mulroony's Volvo."

"Yeah," Will said.

"Sure I did," Eddie said.

"Have you taken her off the island?"

Eddie shook his head. "Nope. You can check the log. My dad usually does the sunrise trip, but I don't recall seeing the Volvo on the log in the past few days."

Will walked to the bow of the ferry and stood at the rail, watching as the island grew on the horizon. Before long, the details of the village were visible. He could see the dock and the Jolly Farmer just beyond, the cobblestone streets and the tiny cottages that were visible along the water to the north and south of the village.

Will was the first one off the ferry and he drove directly to Sorcha's shop and parked on the street in front. He drew a deep breath and gathered his thoughts. His future hinged on this moment, on the first words they said to each other.

He got out of the Mercedes and walked to the shop door, then opened it. The bell above the door jangled as he stepped inside. A moment later, Claire appeared from the rear of the shop, a paintbrush and a rag in her hand. She froze, their gazes locking for a long moment.

"You're here," Will murmured.

"I am," she said.

He chuckled softly. "I'm not sure I want to know what's going on."

"I'm not sure I could tell you," Claire replied. "I just know that I couldn't get on that plane. So Sorcha went home with Eric. And I came back here."

"Why here? Why not the inn?"

"Because I needed a place to stay, a place to figure some things out before I saw you. And Sorcha offered."

"And have you figured everything out?"

"No," Claire said. "But I'm working on it."

"Is there anything I can do to help?" Will asked.

"I'm not sure," she said.

Will crossed the shop in a few long strides. He took Claire's face into his hands and kissed her, softly at first, and then with growing need. He'd thought about this moment over and over, an image of their reunion a constant presence in his head since the day she'd left.

When he finally drew back, he stared down at her beautiful face. A streak of blue paint marred her perfect complexion. "What are you painting?"

Claire took his hand and pulled him along to the back room of the shop. Canvases were propped up along the walls and an easel stood near the windows. "The light in here is the best."

"You've been busy," Will said.

Claire nodded. "For as long as I'm here, I'm going to have to find something useful to do. And since there are no advertising agencies on Trall, I decided to use some of my other talents. I loved to paint at one time."

"Why did you stop?"

"Because it wasn't practical. I couldn't make a living at it, so I focused on things that would pay my rent. But I think I might be good. And maybe now is the time to find out."

Will picked up a canvas and studied it carefully. "It's quite good," he said.

"Are you saying that from an objective viewpoint?" Claire asked. "Or are you saying that because you'd like to kiss me?"

"Who says I want to kiss you?" Will asked. She smiled and he felt a familiar surge of warmth wash over him. That was all it took for him to feel good about his life, just a simple smile from Claire. "I do think it's good, Claire."

"So do I," Claire said. "And it feels good, too. Like it's something I should be doing."

Will chuckled softly. "I've always lived by that adage. If it feels good, do it." He stepped closer. "Now that we've established my credentials as an art critic, would it be all right if I kissed you again?"

Claire shook her head. "I've been thinking…"

"Oh, no," Will said. "That phrase combined with a discussion about sex is never a good thing. You should never think about sex before you have sex. You should just do it."

"We're not going to have sex," Claire said. "That's what I've been thinking about. When I first met you, I decided that it would be fun to have an affair with you. I thought it would be simple to just indulge and then walk away. But that wasn't the case. And now, I need to know that I'm staying for something more than just lust." She paused. "And I want to know that it wasn't the water."

"What does the water have to do with anything?" Will asked.

"Remember that night, after the Samhain celebration? I had a bottle of water in the truck. That was water from the Druid spring."

"But I took the water in the truck the night before," Will said. "That's what I used to make your hangover remedy. I left the empty bottle behind. Not that I believe in the Druid water. In fact, there is some evidence that my great-grandfather is the one who started the legend to help increase tourism on the island."

"Really?" Claire asked.

He nodded. "Not that I'm trying to race past this whole 'getting to know each other' phase. We've both used the water, but I don't think that has anything to do with the way we feel about each other."

"The practical side of me says that's true," Claire replied. "But since I met you, I'm not really sure of anything. Only that I couldn't get on that plane."

Will reached down and grabbed her hand, lacing her fingers through his. "That's a start. And it's enough for me." He leaned forward and kissed her on the cheek. He'd forgotten how good she smelled, sweet and flowery. Will kissed her other cheek. "I'm glad you're here."

He drew back and looked down into her eyes. They watched each other for a long time, neither one of them moving. And then, as if a switch had suddenly been turned on, Claire grabbed him, pulling him against her body.

His mouth found hers and though Will had every intention of respecting her wishes in these matters, it didn't seem as if she was completely committed to celibacy. Her tongue slipped inside his mouth and the kiss became a sensual invitation.

Will reached for the buttons of her paint-stained blouse and a heartbeat later they were both tearing at each other's clothes, fingers fumbling with buttons and zippers. Jeans slid to the floor and were kicked aside, shirts were discarded and underwear pushed away.

He slid his palm along her belly, then lower. She was already slick with desire and Will slipped a finger inside of her. A tiny moan slipped from her lips and she moved against him.

How had he ever imagined doing without this? Will wondered. He craved her body, needed it to live in the same way he needed air to breathe and water to drink. But it wasn't the release that came from sex that he'd grown addicted to. It was the incredible feeling of surrender when he first entered her. He no longer held the power—she did. He trusted her with his heart and his soul.

Claire slid her leg up along his hip, then brushed his hand away, moving against him, his shaft pressed to her belly. But Will was desperate to have her in his arms again. He grabbed her and pulled her up until her legs were wrapped around his waist, then pressed her against the wall.

Her hands clutched at his shoulders and she pushed back until she could look into his eyes. Will drew a ragged breath, taking in her beauty. Her hair tumbled around her face, now flushed pink with desire. A tiny smile curved the corners of her mouth as she shifted in his arms. And then, as if she'd planned it all along, she sank down on top of him, impaling herself on his rigid shaft.

"Ahhh," Will cried, wild sensations shooting through his body. Trying to maintain any kind of control with Claire was impossible. He was always dancing on the edge, a second away from release. It took all his willpower to pull himself back as she began to move above him.

They fit together perfectly. Already, he knew exactly how to move to give her the most pleasure. He cupped her backside in his hands as he thrust into her, each time withdrawing almost completely and then losing himself again. Claire stared down at him, her hair falling over her eyes, her lips swollen from his kiss.

He filled her completely, burying himself to the hilt. There was nothing more he could want from desire, no higher peak he could reach. As long as he had Claire, there would never be another woman. She was the only one who could satisfy him completely and forever.

Claire's eyes were closed now, her brow furrowed in concentration and her lower lip caught between her teeth. He knew the signs, knew that she was close, and Will picked up the pace. She moaned, the sound spurring him on. And then her eyes flew open and she held her breath for a long moment.

She felt hot and wet and wonderfully tight and though he hadn't bothered with a condom, it didn't matter. The last time had been a risk, but now it seemed right that they enjoy each other completely, without anything between them.

Will felt her tighten around him and then dissolve into spasms of pleasure. He couldn't hold back any longer and he joined her, finding his own climax just seconds after hers. His orgasm was powerful, rocking his entire body until he had to focus on remaining upright. His knees felt weak and his limbs boneless. Every muscle that had been flexed before now relaxed, and a delicious sense of completion washed over him.

He slowly lowered her to her feet and then buried his face against the curve of her neck as he caught his breath. "Do you have any idea of what you do to me?"

"It's your fault," Claire answered. "You do it to me. We weren't supposed to do that."

"I'm sorry," he murmured. "We should have used a condom."

"We're covered there," she said. "It's the 'getting to know each other' thing we really messed up."

"All right," Will said, hiding a smile. "From now on, we have to keep our hands off of each other. I promise, I won't touch you unless you touch me. Deal?"

"It's the only way we're going to know for sure."

"Right," Will said, holding his hands up in mock surrender as he stepped back. "I can do that. Really, I can. I promise."

"I'm not blaming you," Claire said. "That was as much my fault as it was yours. We just need to be more determined."

Will bent down to pick up Claire's shirt, then held it out on the end of his finger. He nodded down at her breast, her bra pushed aside to reveal a pink nipple. "You might want to fix that. I'd do it for you, but that would require touching you."

No matter how determined they both were, Will knew it would be impossible to keep their passions in check. "This could get very…uncomfortable."

"Just don't think about it," Claire suggested.

"That might be easy for you to say, but every time I see you, I get hard. You just can't give up sex full stop, especially when the sex is really good."

"You'll just have to take care of those urges yourself," Claire said.

In truth, as long as she was nearby, he wouldn't have any problem in that area. Just closing his eyes and letting an image of her, naked and aroused, drift through his head was enough stimulation to make him come.

But Will didn't think he'd have to wait long. A few days, maybe a week at the outside. Claire was worth each agonizing day. And if it meant she was certain of her feelings for him, then who was he to complain?

Will had no doubts on that score. He knew exactly how he felt about Claire. And when the time was right and when she was ready, then he'd tell her. And then, they'd have the rest of their lives to explore the desires they'd only just touched upon a few minutes before.

THE BELL ABOVE the shop door rang and Claire glanced up from the beads she was stringing to see Mary Kearney step through the door, a small box clutched in her hands. She set down the beads and smiled. "Good morning, Mary," Claire said.

"If it isn't herself," the woman said. "I hear our Will is back. And aren't we all glad."

Claire knew that Mary was only being friendly, but it would take some time to get used to talking about her personal life with her neighbors. "He is," she said. "Has he come by for his raisin scones?"

"He stopped this morning after his run. Told me to bring these over to ye. He knows how much ye love my scones. There's two raisin and two cheese."

"Thank you," Claire said, smiling.

"Thank Will. He's the one who paid for them. I just delivered them." She set the box on the counter. "Your return has been the talk of the town. Everyone is speculatin'. We do love to speculate here on Trall."

Claire opened up the box and pulled out a cheese scone, then nibbled on a corner. "What are people saying?"

"Well, we all love Will and I'm not sure I've ever seen him so happy. That's all to do with ye, I suspect. But we have our worries."

"I see. You think we haven't been spending enough time together?"

"Exactly!" Mary said.

Her idea to "date" Will hadn't been very popular with him. Had he been complaining around the village? Or was Mary just fishing for gossip? It wasn't as if they never saw each other. They'd been out and about in the village, eating dinner at the pub, enjoying a game of darts, walking along Cove Road in the evening when the weather was good and shopping at the market.

"I love living here," Claire said. "And I love the

people on this island. But if you're worrying over our relationship, then you're wasting your time." Claire knew exactly what they were all thinking. She wasn't spending the night at the Ivybrook Inn. And Will wasn't spending the night in Sorcha Mulroony's flat above the shop. So they were left to draw their own conclusions. She'd never even met her neighbors in Chicago, so it would take a bit of time to get used to all the good-hearted meddling.

"Ye like my scones?" Mary asked.

"Yes," Claire said.

"Ye know, I make wedding cakes, too. Keep that in mind. I don't believe there's been a wedding on Trall that I haven't made the cake for. True, there aren't many weddings on Trall. People seem to leave and then get married elsewhere and never come back. Ye can see why we're so excited and hopeful about you and Will."

"Thank you for the offer," Claire said, "but we haven't talked about a wedding. I'm sure you'll hear about it if we do."

"I'm sure I will," Mary said with a wide grin. "Well, I better be off. Take care now, Claire. Stop by for lunch sometime this week."

Claire stared down at the beads and shook her head. There was every chance that the citizens of Trall would know she was getting married to Will before she did. But then, she and Will had been carefully avoiding any talk of the future. For now, she was content to get to know Will outside the bedroom.

Claire smiled to herself. He really was a wonderful man. She'd wondered if some of the attraction between them might fade once they'd decided not to have sex. But it had only become much more intense. Just holding his hand was enough to cause unbidden fantasies to fill her head.

The bell above the door rang again, and this time Annie Mulroony walked in. "Hullo, Claire!"

"Hi, Annie."

"I just thought I'd stop by and tell you Sorcha rang me up this morning. She's having quite the time in New York City. And she's asked me to give you this list. She'd like you to collect some of her things and send them in the post if you could."

Claire took the list and scanned it. She'd become very familiar with Sorcha's closet and recognized the things that she needed. But some of the things on the list were items from the shop. "I'll gather what I can, but you may have to help me with these herbs."

Annie sat down on a stool at the counter and picked up one of the beads Claire had been stringing. "So, everything is going fine with you and Will?"

Claire nodded. "Yes."

"I've noticed that you haven't been spending your nights at the inn. I want you to know that I am a medical professional. If you have any questions or concerns, I'd be happy to advise you, especially on matters of family planning. You realize family planning was against the law here in Ireland until just recently."

"I have that covered for now," Claire said.

"Good, good. Because everyone on the island is very excited about the possibility of having a little Donovan running about. And let me assure you, if you decide not to have the baby here on the island, the hospital in Limerick is lovely. And I wouldn't be insulted at all, even though I have helped bring two hundred and fourteen citizens of Trall into this world."

"I'll keep that in mind," Claire said. Now this was going too far! The next person through the door would probably volunteer to plan her child's tenth birthday party.

"I only wish Sorcha were still here. You two would have made such good friends. Odd though, how you both ended up with the other's man. There's a lovely symmetry to that, isn't there? Hmmm. Well, I'd better be gone. I have patients."

The next time the bell above the door rang, Claire was ready to tell whomever it was to mind their own business. But Will poked his head in the door and grinned. "I'm going over to the bakery. Can I get you a coffee or a cup of tea?"

She held up the box of scones. "Mary Kearney stopped by with food and an offer to make our wedding cake. And then Annie Mulroony was here giving me family planning advice."

"Sorry," Will said, stepping inside. "That's just the way things work on Trall. Everyone says they mind their own business and never gossip, but they consider it their civic duty to comment on everyone else's business. They say we're having problems in the bedroom."

Claire giggled. "It's causing a bit of concern on Trall, the fact that we aren't spending our nights together."

Will circled the counter and slipped his arms around Claire's waist. He pulled her against him, bringing their hips together in a way that Claire found quite provocative. She shifted and Will groaned. "If you expect me to follow your rules, then I don't think it's fair to provoke me."

"Sorry," Claire said. "It's just that we decided on a plan and I'd like to see it through."

"You're not going to let me get to second base?" Will asked. He slipped his hands beneath her shirt and rubbed the small of her back. "I could always ignore the rules and skip third and go right to fourth."

"There is no fourth base," Claire said.

"I thought fourth base was sex."

"No, that's a home run."

"Is that so?"

"Yes. Home plate is a different shape entirely. It looks like a little house and bases are like square bags and—"

Will brought his mouth down on hers, the rest of her words stilled by his kiss. His hands caressed her face and he smoothed her hair back as he dropped a trail of kisses across her cheek to her ear. Claire drew back and forced a smile. "You should probably go."

"How long are we going to do this?" Will asked. "It seems a bit pointless to me."

"That's because all you think about is sex. We need to stick to the plan and get to know each other a little better before we hop back into bed."

"I'm making supper for you tonight at the inn. And we'll discuss second base in more detail then. In fact, you can tell me more about baseball in general."

"Baseball is really hard to explain," Claire said. "It would be easier if we watched a game."

Will dropped a kiss on Claire's nose, then walked to the door. He glanced back over his shoulder. "I'll see you tonight. Seven. Don't be late."

The moment the door closed, Claire locked it. It was time. It had been time since the moment Will had returned to Trall and walked in the door of the shop, but she'd convinced herself that abstinence was the only way to know for sure.

She was in love with Will Donovan and sex or no sex, that wasn't going to change. So what in the world was she doing sleeping alone every night? From now on, she'd be spending her nights in Will's bed, in his arms.

Claire ran her hands through her hair. She wanted a nap and a nice long bath and plenty of time to get ready. A flutter of nerves gripped her stomach. Sex had always been so natural between them, something they'd enjoyed without thinking a whole lot about it.

"There will be a home run on Trall tonight," Claire murmured to herself. "And I'm going to hit it."

9

"CODDLE? YOU MADE CODDLE. Don't you think you might have chosen a better menu for a romantic dinner?" Katie wrinkled her nose as she picked up the lid on the pot and looked inside. "I could have made you a lovely beef Wellington or roasted lamb. Coddle is what you serve when you have the lads over to watch football."

Will shook his head. "Sausages, potatoes and onions can be perfectly romantic in the right setting," he said. He grabbed a bottle of Guinness and held it up. "Especially when paired with the right brand of beer."

"Are you trying to drive her off the island?" Katie asked. "We all love Claire and if you do anything to bollocks this up, Will Donovan, you're not going to have many friends left on Trall."

"I know what I'm doing," Will said. "And the lot of you can stop worrying about my personal life."

"It's just that you and Claire seemed so close and then she left and you left and she came back and you came back and it hasn't been the same since then. You don't…well, she doesn't…I'm only makin' one side of your bed, if you get my meaning."

"We're just taking some time," Will said. "And you can let everyone know that I'm doing my best to convince Claire to stay on the island."

"Good," Katie said. "But I still say you won't do it with Dublin coddle." She grabbed her jacket from the back of one of the kitchen stools and Will held it out for her. "There's an apple pie in the freezer. Put it in to warm before you serve dinner. At least you can give the girl a decent dessert." She turned and buttoned up her jacket. "And light a few candles. It wouldn't hurt to make the place a bit more romantic."

"Thank you," Will said, walking her to the back door. When he'd closed it behind her, he glanced down at his watch. Claire was due in ten minutes, just enough time to put on his most faded pair of jeans and an old T-shirt.

The past two weeks had been absolute torture. Though he agreed to Claire's master plan, it had only taken a few hours for him to realize that going backward in their relationship was impossible. They'd shared the most intimate experiences together, she'd touched him like no other woman had before. And Will wanted to relive those experiences over and over again.

The only thing that had kept him sane through this period of celibacy was the knowledge that when they finally did make love, it would be incredibly intense. And he was willing to make this compromise if the end result would be Claire—in his life, and his bed, forever.

But two weeks was long enough. Tonight, they'd sleep in the same bed again. And it would be Claire's idea, not his. His plan was a bit devious, but he was tired of wasting time. The best way to make her want him was if his own interest in sex began to wane.

Will walked back to his room and rummaged through the clean laundry for his jeans. When he was dressed, he stood in front of the bathroom mirror and messed up his hair. He hadn't bothered to shave in the last three days. It wouldn't do to put too much effort into his appearance. When he looked properly rumpled, Will walked back to the kitchen and opened a bottle of Guinness.

"Hello?"

"I'm back here," Will called at the sound of her voice. "In the kitchen."

A few moments later, Claire walked in. Her hair had been tousled by the brisk wind blowing across the island and her cheeks were a pretty shade of pink. Will walked over to her and helped her out of her jacket, then bent forward and placed a chaste kiss on her cheek. "How was your day, dear?" he asked.

Claire slowly turned to face him. It took every ounce of willpower not to capture her mouth and give her the kind of kiss he'd been fantasizing about all day long, deep and wet and stirring. But he was nothing if not resolved to stick to *his* plan…and his plan was to ruin *her* plan.

"It was fine," Claire said. "I packed up some things to send to Sorcha. And I worked on some jewelry for the shop. I started a new painting. And then I got ready to come here."

"You look lovely," Will said, taking in the gauzy cotton top with the beaded neckline. The fabric was almost transparent and he recognized the pretty lace bra she wore. He'd removed that bra more than once, but it had been far too long since he'd touched what was underneath.

A tiny smile curved the corners of her lush mouth at his compliment. She plucked at the shirt. "Thank you. It's not mine. I found it in Sorcha's closet."

"If you're planning to stay on the island, you should probably send for some of your things," Will suggested.

"Probably," she responded. Claire strolled over to the cooker and peeked at the contents of the pot. "What are we having for dinner?"

"Nothing special," Will said. "Would you like a beer? I've got Guinness."

"Do you have wine?" Claire asked. "I saw a bottle of champagne in the fridge. Maybe we could have that?"

"I was saving that for something special," Will said. God, he felt like a real shit, but a man had to do what a man had to do. He grabbed an open bottle of white and poured her a glass. "Hey, I thought we might play some games, just to pass the time."

"Games?" She swallowed hard. "I do remember you were pretty good at 'I Never'."

"I've laid out the Scrabble board. I thought we might have a game before dinner."

Claire reached for her wineglass, a frown creasing her brow. "You want to play Scrabble?"

Will saw the look of disappointment in her eyes. Was she expecting more? If she was, then she'd have to be the one to suggest it. "You'd mentioned you liked to play. Or we can play backgammon."

"No," Claire said with a forced smile. "Scrabble will be…fun."

Will rubbed his hands together. "Good. I'm ready to play then."

They walked through the inn to the parlor. Will had set the board on a small mahogany card table near the fireplace. He pulled out Claire's chair, then sat down across from her. "You know, it's really nice that we can spend a quiet evening at home without thinking about…you know."

"What?"

"Well, sex," he said. He tried to keep a straight face. "In fact, I haven't really thought about sex in at least a week, maybe more. This plan of yours has really taught me to put my priorities in order regarding our relationship."

"It has?"

Will knew his toying with her had to be confusing. But it was time she realized that planning out every facet of their lives would never work. When they were together, they were driven by their desires and passions, and not by some blueprint Claire had sketched out for a successful relationship.

"I love Scrabble," Will said. "We should make this a regular thing. Every Saturday night could be Scrabble night. Doesn't that sound like a good plan?"

"Well, not every Saturday night. Sometimes, we might want to do something else."

"Maybe. But if we don't have anything better to do, then Scrabble is fun." He held out the sack of tiles. "Go ahead. Closest to *A* goes first." Claire took the honors and they each grabbed seven tiles.

"Pen," Claire said, placing her tiles on the board. "Ten points." She wrote the score on a notepad and grabbed three new tiles from the bag.

"And I'm going to add an *I* and an *S*. Penis," Will said. "That's eight, plus double word score is sixteen."

"No, it's not a double word score. You can't use that square because that was used on my play."

"Irish rules," Will said.

Claire frowned. "All right. Soap. Seven points."

Will stared at his tiles, then picked two up. "Sex," he said as he placed the tiles using the *E* from *penis*. "That's double letter scores on the *S* and the *X*. Nineteen."

Claire frowned. "I can see where your mind is tonight."

"Not at all," Will countered. "It's funny, but I'm not even thinking about that. It's just the letters I'm pulling from the bag."

"You aren't thinking about sex?"

He shook his head. "Your turn."

"Why aren't you thinking about sex?" Claire asked. "Just because we're not having sex doesn't mean you can't think about it."

Will studied his tiles. "I'm better off putting it out of my head completely. It's quite simple. In fact, I don't really miss it at all."

Claire turned her attention back to her tiles. After a minute, she placed a word on the board. "Green. Seven points."

"Orgasm," Will said as he placed his tiles on the board. "Double word score, that's twenty. Too bad I didn't have an *I* and a *C*. I could have gotten a fifty point bonus for using all my letters."

"Are you cheating?" Claire asked.

"How does one cheat at Scrabble?" Will asked. "It's a legitimate word. Oh, wait, I'm not done." He added an *S*. "Orgasms. Multiple. That's twenty-two." He grabbed the score pad from Claire. "So, how am I doing here? You have twenty-four points and I have fifty-seven."

Claire glared at him through narrowed eyes. "Ask. *A-S-K*. Triple letter score on the *K*, that's seventeen."

"Blow," Will said, placing his next word. "And that's just ten. Too bad I didn't have—"

"What? *J-O-B?* You know, I'm really not in the mood for Scrabble," Claire said.

"Would you like to play backgammon? Or chess? Do you know chess?"

She shook her head. "Maybe we could just sit and talk?" She got up and sat on one end of the sofa and patted the spot beside her. "Let's just relax."

Will didn't accept her invitation, but instead sank into one of the overstuffed chintz chairs, stretching his legs out in front of him. "The weather was nice today, wasn't it? Not too cold. Usually there's more rain this time of year." Talking about the weather was sure to push her over the edge. Will couldn't think of anything more boring than the weather on Trall in late-November. Rain, wind, rain, wind, and occasionally, a little sleet.

"I wouldn't know, since this is my first November on Trall."

"Right," Will said, nodding his head. "Did you hear that Mary Kearney is going to paint the bakery and tea shop? She tells me she wants to go with a pale blue."

Claire stood up, smoothing her hands along her hips. "You know, I have a bit of a headache."

"Would you like an aspirin?"

"No, no. It's probably the wine. I think I'm just tired. Maybe I should just…go to bed."

This was an interesting development, Will mused. Was she waiting for him to invite her to his bed? "That would probably be for the best," he finally said. "Would you like me to drive you home?"

"No," Claire snapped. "I can get home on my own, thanks."

"I could send some supper with you. You might be hungry later."

She shook her head. "I—I'll talk to you tomorrow, Will."

Will watched as she walked back to the kitchen to grab her jacket. A few moments later, he heard the back door slam and he chuckled to himself. "That went well," he murmured with a soft chuckle.

Perhaps it wasn't playing fair. But if he didn't force the issue with Claire, they might go on like this for months. He was not cut out to be Claire O'Connor's friend. From the moment they'd met, they'd been drawn to each other in a powerfully sexual way and that was nothing to be ashamed of. He loved everything about Claire, including her body.

Will glanced at his watch. He was certain she'd return. She'd go back to Sorcha's, begin thinking about their evening together, and after an hour or two, decide she'd had enough. And then, they could finally begin the rest of their lives together.

CLAIRE THREW the Volvo into gear and sped out of the driveway of the inn, the car skidding in the gravel. She wasn't sure whether to laugh or cry. Wasn't this exactly what she was protecting herself against?

When she'd come back to Trall, she'd been determined to figure out whether her relationship with Will was meant to last. She'd been fooled once with Eric and Claire couldn't think of anything worse that getting caught up in a one-sided love affair again. But now, her worst fears had come to pass. Will was losing interest.

"You should be happy," she muttered as she drove back toward the village. "You found out before he could break your heart—completely." In truth, if this was the end, then her heart would be broken. But she wouldn't play the fool as she had with Eric. At least, she'd have saved herself from complete humiliation.

But where did this leave her? She'd cast aside her life in the States to stay here on the island. Eric had probably already hired another art director. Beyond her family, there was nothing left for her in Chicago. This was exactly why she'd walked away in the first place. A girl just doesn't move halfway across the world for a guy she barely knows.

Claire pulled the car up behind Sorcha's shop and then climbed the stairs to the second-floor flat. When she got inside, she threw off her jacket, kicked off her shoes and climbed under the bedcovers. She'd laid such a careful plan with Eric and their relationship had ended badly after three years. Another careful plan with Will had left her with a grand total of just under a month. At that rate, her next relationship should last approximately thirty-three seconds, give or take.

Claire curled up beneath the covers and closed her eyes. Images of Will, naked and aroused, swirled in her head. It felt like ages since they'd made love, but it had only been a couple weeks. Even now, thinking about what they had done together caused a wave of desire to course through her body. They'd been so…perfect.

Maybe she should have gotten on the plane and gone back to New York. Perhaps her instincts had been right all along. This had been nothing more than just a vacation fling, a fiery affair that was bound to run out of fuel. Claire groaned and pulled the pillow over her head. But even as the thought formed in her mind, Claire knew in her heart that it couldn't be true. What they'd shared was much more than sex. There had been a deeper connection, something more profound.

The sound of the phone split the silence and Claire tumbled off the bed. At first, she didn't want to answer it. What if it was Will? But then, her grandmother preferred to call around nine at night, which was right after watching Oprah and right before she began dinner preparations. Claire reached for the phone.

"Hello?"

"Claire! Hello from America."

Claire recognized Sorcha's voice. "Hi, Sorcha."

"I hoped you weren't asleep. I didn't wake you, did I?"

"It's only nine p.m. here," Claire said.

"I'm so bad with this time difference," she said. "This is what comes from living in one place my whole life."

"How is New York?"

"Oh, it's still wonderful. It snowed yesterday and this coming week is your Thanksgiving. Eric says I have to cook a turkey. What is this American obsession with turkey. Is it some kind of holy icon?"

"Have Eric tell you about the Pilgrims," Claire said.

"I saw one the other day on the street, passing out adverts for mobile phones. I asked him if he knew how to cook a turkey and he looked at me like I was daft. I may need to call you for advice."

"I'm always here," Claire said.

"Oh, and I rode the tube yesterday and got to where I wanted to go. And we've been to the Statue of Liberty and to the top of the Empire State Building. I love the pizza. I can't understand why you Americans just don't eat that for Thanksgiving."

"And how is Eric?"

"He's fine. He's been so sweet to me, Claire. He took me out for a wonderful dinner at a little restaurant in the village. That's Greenwich Village."

"Yes, I know," Claire said.

"And he's introduced me to his friends. How are things with Will? Have you married him yet? I'll be crushed if you don't ask me to be a bridesmaid. Or better yet, I'll perform the ceremony."

Claire paused. Emotion welled up in her throat. "Actually, things aren't going so well. I think he's losing interest. I probably should have gotten on that plane with you and Eric."

"Will?" Sorcha laughed. "Oh, please. He's madly in love with you. You could grow a big wart on the end of your nose tomorrow and he'd still think you were the most beautiful woman in the world."

"We've just been trying to take our relationship a bit slower, so we get to know each other as friends first."

"Bloody hell, why would you do that?" Sorcha asked.

"I just thought it would be…" Claire sighed. "It was stupid. I know. But in the beginning everything moved so fast. And now, he's lost interest. In sex. And in me."

"You can't know that for sure," Sorcha said. "He might just be in a mood. Maybe you'll have to snap him out of it."

"How will I do that?"

"Go over to the inn, take off all your clothes and crawl into bed with him. I'm sure you'll both be right as rain before the sun comes up. And if not, I've got a few bottles of the Druid water in the cabinet above the kitchen sink. Just give him a cup of tea and he'll be all over you."

The Druid water is what had gotten her into this mess in the first place. She wasn't about to use it again. "I'm not going to do that," Claire said.

"Suit yourself. But if you two aren't meant for each other, then I don't know who is."

"Maybe I should go talk to him. I can't stand all this confusion. If it's really over, then I want to know so I can get on with my life."

"Do it right now, tonight. And after you've had a pleasant night of hot, animal sex, could you find my blue beaded coat and my black lace-up boots and put them in the post for me? Or better yet, give them to my mother. She's been sending me all the little things I can't get over here, like my favorite soap and my favorite marmalade."

"I'll do that."

"You know, I could probably try to do a spell. But I'm not sure how to deal with the distance. Would you like me to give it a go?"

"No, I'm going to have to deal with this on my own," Claire said.

They chatted for a few more minutes before Claire said goodbye and hung up. She glanced around the flat, the cozy interior suddenly so cold and unwelcoming. Grabbing her jacket, Claire headed to the door. It was time to settle this. If Will was losing interest, then there was no reason for her to stay on Trall.

It took her only five minutes to get back to the inn. She parked the Volvo out front and then hurried to the door. But to her surprise, Will had locked it again. "Damned locked doors!" she screamed. Clenching her fingers into a fist, she pounded on the door until her hand hurt.

A few moments later, the front light went on and Will opened the door. He was shirtless and barefoot and it was obvious he'd just pulled on his jeans. "It took you long enough," he murmured, running his hand through his hair and squinting at her through sleepy eyes. He grabbed her elbow and dragged her inside, then closed the door behind her.

"We need to talk," Claire said, trying to control the emotion in her voice.

He sighed deeply. "No, we don't." He took her face in his hands and kissed her, his mouth warm and damp on hers, his tongue slipping between her lips to tease and taste. The kiss went on and on, until Claire was breathless and light-headed. When he finally drew away, she gasped.

"There, that's much better." He turned and walked toward the dining room. "Are you coming?"

"Coming where?" Claire asked.

"To bed," Will said. He turned around and faced her. "That's why you're here, isn't it?"

"I came here to talk to you. About us."

"No, no. We're not going to talk. We're going to crawl into bed and you're going to have your way with me. Or I'll have my way with you. We can talk in the morning."

"You can't force me to go to bed with you!" Claire cried.

"I'm not forcing you to do anything," Will said. "I'm inviting you, Claire. If you come to bed with me, I promise, you won't regret it."

"But what about our plan?"

"You mean *your* plan? I don't want to do that anymore. I hate your plan. I have plenty of friends, Claire, and I occasionally have a pint down at the pub with them. When I think of you, I don't think of you as a mate. At least not in the platonic sense. You're the woman I love."

"You love me?"

"Of course I do. If I didn't, I wouldn't have put up with this silly plan of yours for two feckin' weeks. I want you with me, every day and every night. I don't want to play Scrabble and I don't want to talk about the damn weather. I want to lie in bed with you in my arms and be completely and utterly happy. Now what's wrong with that?"

"Nothing," Claire breathed.

"Good. Then I think it's time we made a new plan. I think we should plan not to have a plan."

Claire considered the suggestion. Things had gone so much better between them when they had depended on sheer spontaneity, that much was true. "I—I guess we could try that," Claire said.

Will stared at her for a long moment, then smiled. "Come to bed with me, Claire." He held out his hand and she slowly approached him.

His gaze was fixed on her face and she saw the desire there. A warm flush washed over her body and her nerves prickled in anticipation of his touch. Trembling, she placed her fingers in his palm.

Will led her back to his apartment, through the dimly lit sitting room and into his bedroom. He sat on the edge of the bed and slowly stripped off her clothes, dropping each item onto the floor.

He rose to stand in front of her, then undid his jeans and let them fall to his feet. "This is the way it should be between us," he murmured, cupping her breast in his hand. He bent to tease at her nipple with his tongue.

"I'm sorry," Claire whispered, running her fingers through his hair and holding him close. "I got scared. And I get really stupid when I get scared."

Will wrapped his arms around her waist and looked into her eyes, his lips damp and curved into a tiny smile. "Thank God for that. Coming to Trall was pretty stupid, but it was the best thing that ever happened to me."

"It was?"

"You don't have to be scared. I would never hurt you. I swear. Never."

"I kept thinking of all the reasons why this couldn't work, why I had to protect myself. But I still wanted to believe we'd be together forever."

He pressed a kiss to the curve of her neck. "You shouldn't think so much," Will said.

"Don't you think about us?"

"I think about how soft your skin is and how I love to hear you laugh and how nice it is to kiss you whenever I want. How beautiful you look without clothes—and with clothes, too. I think about how smart you are and how you always manage to look at things in such a unique way, a way that shows me who you are, deep inside." He paused. "But mostly, when I'm around you, I don't think, I just feel."

"I really messed things up, didn't I?"

"Nothing that can't be fixed," Will said. "My feelings haven't changed in two weeks. Have yours?"

Claire shook her head. "No."

"There. That wasn't so hard, was it?" He gathered her in his arms and held her tight. "So was it the Scrabble or was it the discussion of the weather?"

She tipped her head back and laughed. "Actually, it was the comment about Mary Kearney painting the bakery blue that frightened me."

"Interesting," Will said.

"You knew I'd come back tonight, didn't you? You were waiting."

"I hoped you'd come back. And if you didn't, I was

going to show up at Sorcha's sometime before midnight and crawl into your bed."

"I'd much rather be here. The bed is so much bigger. And more comfortable." She frowned. "Didn't you promise this bed to Sorcha?"

"She took Eric instead," he replied.

Will spanned her waist with his hands and boosted her up onto the bed, then flopped down beside her, his leg tangled between hers. Slowly, they began to touch each other, finding all the favorite spots that tingled with pleasure.

He was hard and hot and when Claire wrapped her fingers around his shaft, a long sigh slipped from his lips. Slowly, she began to stroke him, at first in an easy rhythm. Will, in turn, found the center of her desire, gently rubbing her with his thumb.

But Claire wasn't satisfied to just touch him. She rolled over and straddled his hips with her legs. Will stared at her, his eyes glazed with desire. She teased at her damp entrance with the tip of his shaft and then, when he groaned, Claire slowly sank down on top of him.

"Oh," he breathed. "See. This is what we are. Perfect. Together. Just like this."

She began to move above him, pulling away until he was nearly outside of her, then dropping back down. She controlled the pace and the depth of his penetration and Claire could see that he was trying not to surrender. She bent closer and ran her tongue along his lower lip.

Will slipped his hand through her hair and held her there, caught in a deep and powerful kiss. But that only seemed to drive him closer to the edge. He grabbed her hips and tried to keep her from moving, but Claire only wanted his complete surrender.

"Don't," he said, as she continued to rise and fall above him. "Oh, God, Claire. Slow down."

"No," she moaned. "I can't. I need you too much."

She kissed him again and then she felt every muscle in his body tense. An instant later, he dissolved in an explosive orgasm, his body shuddering and shaking with each deep thrust.

Claire collapsed on top of him, nestling her face into the curve of his neck. She drew a deep breath, inhaling the scent of him. Until this moment, she'd never truly believed that they'd spend the rest of their lives together. But now she could imagine it.

All of her dreams for her life—the upwardly mobile husband with the well-paying job, the two children in private school, the big house in the suburbs—all of that seemed part of a different lifetime. Perhaps it was another woman's dream, a woman she'd left behind the moment she'd set foot on Trall.

Will slowly smoothed his palm over her hair. "Are we all right now?" he asked.

"Yes," Claire said, smiling. She pushed up on her elbow and looked down into his beautiful eyes. "We're just fine."

WILL FILLED a small glass with orange juice, then grabbed the toast and slathered on a spoonful of strawberry preserves. Though he'd tried to convince Claire of the benefits of a proper Irish breakfast—eggs and sausage, bacon and soda farl, and of course, potatoes—she always preferred something simpler.

He smiled to himself. It was nice knowing these little things about her, like how she fluffed up her pillow before she slept and how she twisted a lock of her hair when she was reading. They weren't important things, but they were things that he noticed.

And she did love to sleep late. It was nearly ten and Will usually started his day at dawn. They'd slept an hour or two last night, but he felt alive, energized, as if he could run ten miles without breaking a sweat.

They'd spent most of the night in the midst of one seduction or another, each one ending only when one of them was spent. In truth, Will wondered how long they'd be able to go on without one of them requiring medical attention. He was looking forward to finding out.

There didn't seem to be a limit to their desire for each other. Every time they touched, Will wanted more. He could never know her body completely, never know how she'd react to each new way of making love.

He wanted a future with her and he'd do anything to make that happen. His trip to Dublin had been an escape, but he'd also considered a few job opportunities there. Though he was already independently wealthy, with enough money to last for many years to come, he needed a profession, something to occupy his mind beyond thinking about Claire twenty-four-seven.

As for Claire, she needed something to satisfy her own ambitions. She'd thrown herself into her painting and was excited about improving on her talents. But there were only so many pretty scenes on the island and a limited number of patrons who might buy her paintings. In order for her to be successful at anything, they'd need to leave Trall.

He'd been mulling over all of their options. There was Dublin, if they wanted to stay in Ireland, with weekends at the country house in County Kerry. There was always London, if Claire wanted something a bit more sophisticated, or even Paris, the center of the art world. They could return to the States. Will would be more than happy living in Chicago, as long as he was there with Claire. Or New York.

The teakettle on the stove whistled and Will scooped some dry tea into a china pot, then filled it with water. But before he could pick up the tray, he heard the bell for the front door. It was just past ten on a Monday morning. There were no reservations so he suspected that Dickie O'Malley was stopping by for his once-monthly bath.

Will jogged through the dining room, unlocked the door and pulled it open. But instead of finding Trall's most notorious serial bather, he found an elderly woman standing on the steps, her luggage at her feet. "Good morning," Will said.

She peered up at him, studying Will's face with an inscrutable expression. "Are you himself, then?"

"That depends," Will said.

"Are you the man who has stolen my granddaughter from me?"

Will's breath caught in his throat. "Oh, you're talking about Claire. Are you Orla O'Connor?"

"I am," she said.

She was a tiny woman, just a few inches over five

feet, with snow-white hair and a slender figure. But she had a way of looking at him, staring at him with a steely glare, that caused Will to squirm. She was the closest thing to a parent Claire had in Ireland and her disapproval was obvious. He wasn't sure how she'd feel about finding Claire naked in his bed, but he suspected she wouldn't be thrilled.

"You've come a long way, Mrs. O'Connor." Will pulled the door open and stepped back to allow her to enter. She wandered inside and he grabbed her bags and brought them in as well, arranging them in a neat little row at the door.

"I stopped at that shop in town and Claire wasn't there. I don't suppose she'd be here, then, would she?"

"She is," Will said. "Would you like me to get her?"

"No," Orla said. "I think I'd like to speak with you first."

"I've just brewed a pot of tea. Why don't you come into the dining room and we'll have a bit of breakfast. Then I'll show you to your room. You will be staying for a time, won't you?"

Orla frowned, looking entirely displeased with him. "You are charming, I'll give you that."

It sounded much more like an insult than a compliment, Will thought. "Claire has talked so much about you. I'm anxious to know you better." He showed her to a table, pulling out her chair for her, then hurried to the kitchen. The tray with Claire's breakfast was still sitting on the worktable. Will grabbed it and carried it in to her grandmother, setting it down on a corner of the table.

"Here's tea," he said, as he poured her a cup. "And there's toast. The preserves are from strawberries grown on the island."

"You're handy in the kitchen?" Orla asked.

"I do my best. We serve breakfast here at the inn and I help our cook."

Orla took a sip of her tea and glanced around the room. "Where is Claire?"

Will hesitated, then realized that Grandmother O'Connor was far too astute to fool with bald-faced lies and silly excuses. "She's still asleep. We had a late night last night. I can wake her if you'd like."

"I'd assume she's sleeping in your bed?"

Will cleared his throat. "You'd assume correctly."

Claire's grandmother took another sip of her tea. "I can't say that I could resist the charms of man as handsome as yourself. If I were only a few years younger."

"Just a few," Will teased. That brought a smile and Will claimed a small victory from it. Already, he could see where Claire got her beauty, and her direct nature. She and her grandmother were cut from the same cloth.

"And I do know the effects of drinking the water on this island. That's how I got my husband to marry me," she said.

"Interesting," Will said.

"Let me get right to the point," Orla continued. "What are your intentions, Mr. Donovan?"

Will hadn't ever really set them out in words. He considered her question for a moment, then decided to answer as plainly as he could. "I intend to marry your granddaughter just as soon as she'll have me. But after what happened with Eric, I think she might need some time before we make it official. I'll give her all the time she needs. Once we do marry, I hope to have a family with her and make her happy for the rest of her life."

"And where will you live?"

"Wherever Claire wants to live," Will replied. He hadn't thought about it until that morning, but where they lived made absolutely no difference to him. Though he loved Ireland, his love of the country didn't come close to the love he had for Claire. "It makes no difference to me. I have the means to live anywhere."

Orla nodded curtly. "It seems you have all the proper answers to my questions."

"That's good, isn't it?"

She smiled again, this time more warmly. "That's very good. Now, I'd like to freshen up a bit before I see my granddaughter. I want you to give me your best room and then I want you to wake up Claire and tell her she has a visitor."

"She'll be happy to see you," Will said.

"Of course she will," Orla replied. "I'm her favorite grandmother."

Will took Orla upstairs and put her in the room that Claire had first occupied. Before he left, he started a fire in the fireplace and placed her bags on the window seat. "I hope you'll be very comfortable here," he said.

"It brings back memories," Orla said with a melancholy smile. "It seems like just yesterday, I rode the boat over here. I was so young then. I had my whole life before me." She sat down on the edge of the bed. "I thought we'd have forever together."

Will saw tears swimming in her eyes and he sat down beside her and took her hand. Orla clutched at his hand, squeezing it tight. "I lost my dear husband five years ago. And even after forty-five years together, it wasn't enough." She turned to Will. "Don't waste a single day, not a single day. You'll never get it back."

"So the water worked for you?" Will said.

"There are times when every romance needs a bit of magic, Mr. Donovan," she said. "Real or imagined, it doesn't matter. When we're in love we're willing to grasp at any straw to believe it will be forever."

Will leaned closer and kissed her cheek. He suspected that Grandfather O'Connor hadn't stood a chance once Orla set her heart on him. If only Claire were as certain about her feelings.

Will left Orla to unpack, then hurried back downstairs. When he returned to his bedroom, he found Claire still buried beneath the down comforter. He crawled up on the bed and lay down beside her, kissing her once and then again. When she didn't stir, Will gave her a gentle shake.

Claire groaned. "Go away. It's too early to get up."

"You said you wanted to talk," Will said. "It's morning now and I think we should talk."

Claire opened her eyes and regarded him suspiciously. "You want to talk now?"

"I know how much you love your career. And I'm really not tied to the island. My sister and her husband have talked about taking over the inn. So, I was thinking we might want to consider relocating. I have a lot of professional possibilities. I don't have to work, if I don't want to, but if I do, I can come and go from almost anywhere. And—"

"Stop," Claire said, pushing the hair out of her eyes. She sniffed, then wrinkled her nose. "What is that smell?"

Will blinked. "I don't smell anything."

"I do," Claire said. She sniffed again. "Oh, can't you smell that?"

Will lifted his arm, but he'd remembered deodorant after his morning shower. His hair was clean and his teeth were brushed. Had he left something in the oven? Was there a gas leak? "What does it smell like?"

"Hmmm," Claire said. "It smells like…a plan."

Will laughed. "Yes, I suppose you're right. I'm sorry. I don't know what got into me. Lack of sleep?"

She reached out and smoothed her hand over his cheek. "Let's just see where life takes us," Claire said. "I'm happy right now and I'm content to stay here, with you, and run this inn. But if something more interesting comes along, we'll talk about it then. I don't want our plans to ruin our life together."

"All right, we won't make plans. But is there anything you think you might like to do within the next month or two?"

"I'd like to go home to Chicago. I need to move out of my apartment. And I'd like to introduce you to my family."

"That would be nice," Will said. "Although, I've already met your grandmother."

"Did she call?" Claire sat up. "I talked to her a few days ago. She wasn't happy."

"She seems good now," Will said. "I gave her the nicest room and she's upstairs resting a bit. I told her you'd come up and see her as soon as you were dressed."

Claire raked her hand though her tangled hair, the comforter falling away from her naked breasts. "My grandmother is here?"

"She arrived on the first ferry. She told me she'd come to fetch you. But I explained I wasn't going to let you go so easily. We came to an agreement."

"And what was that?" Clare said, smiling.

"As long as my intentions were honorable, she wouldn't try to convince you to leave."

"And are they? Honorable?"

"Some of them are. And the rest are entirely improper. But I'm going to let you sort them out on your own, in your own time." He grabbed her hand. "Come on. You need to get dressed. She's come a long way to convince you that I'm some sort of ruthless bounder. And I think you ought to convince her otherwise."

"She's always looked out for me," Claire said. "I was always her favorite."

"Then we have something in common," Will said.

He watched from the bed as Claire collected her clothes. When she went into the bathroom to take a quick shower, he stood against the sink and chatted with her. And when she emerged, he took a fluffy towel and dried her naked body.

This was what life was supposed to be like, he mused. Taking joy in the simple things, knowing that he was with the one person who was meant for him and him alone. Whatever the circumstances that had brought them together, it didn't matter. They'd found each other in this great big world. And it seemed right that they'd build a life together.

Epilogue

CLAIRE STOOD on the busy street in the Wicker Park neighborhood of Chicago. She and Will had been back for nearly a week, visiting her parents and grandmother, seeing some of the sights and staying in a lovely suite at the Drake.

Will had been gone all morning and Claire had received a phone message from the front desk that she was to meet him at this address. But she'd expected a restaurant and a quiet lunch, just the two of them, not an abandoned brick warehouse.

They'd been back to the States at least once every three or four months since Claire had officially set up residence in Ireland. Though she loved Trall, there were times when she grew homesick for her hometown. There was no place to get a decent pizza in Ireland, and they didn't have a Thai restaurant that delivered to Trall, and she missed her favorite neighborhood coffee shop. Espresso from the machine Will had bought her just wasn't the same as grabbing her double Americano every morning on her way to work.

But there were many more benefits to living with Will. Every day was an adventure, something new and exciting, even if they were just painting the parlor or raking the lawn. When they weren't at home, they traveled. He'd shown her all his favorite spots in Europe and they'd spent some time in New Zealand and Japan while he was doing some consulting work. They'd vacationed in the Caribbean and next month were planning a trip to Egypt.

Claire loved their footloose existence, but she'd been thinking more and more about settling down in one spot. About finally getting married and starting a family.

"Claire!"

She spun around to see Will standing in a doorway near the corner of the building. "What's going on?" she asked.

"You have to see this place," he said. "It's perfect." He strode out into the noonday sunshine and grabbed her hand. "Come on. I know you're going to love it."

"What are we doing here?" she asked.

"Wait. You'll see."

They walked up a short, dark stairwell into the dusty interior. Light filtered in from windows high on each wall, illuminating the dust motes kicked up by Will's footsteps. From what Claire could see, there wasn't much to see. The windows were cloudy with dust and dirt, the building smelled musty and old, and it was nothing but open space with brick pillars holding up the second story.

"What do you think?" Will said.

"About what?"

"This place."

Claire glanced around. "It's a wreck. Why are we here?"

"Because I wanted your opinion. What do you think? Is this good?

"Good for what?"

"For us. I need office space here in the States for my consulting business. And you need loft space to paint. And we need a place to live while we're here. We can turn the upstairs into an apartment and use the ground floor for work."

"We're staying in Chicago?"

"Only if you want to," Will said. "I know how much you miss your family, Claire, and there's no reason why we can't spend more time here. I can live anywhere as long as there's a decent airport close by. I think we could be happy here."

He looked so desperate for her approval. "And you've already bought it," Claire said with a smile.

"I signed the papers this morning. There was another offer, I had no choice. So please tell me you like it. Or I'll be stuck with a shabby old warehouse and not a potential home for us."

Claire wrapped her arms around his neck and kissed him gently. "I love it. It's perfect. And if we have a place here, then we can come and go as we please. No more hotel suites."

"Just a home," Will said.

A home, Claire mused. They'd been together for almost a year and a half now and anywhere they slept had always been their home. They'd never had an idea of where they might be from week to week. But perhaps it was time to start a new era in their lives together.

"I love our life," Claire said. "It's perfect in every way."

"I know a way it could be more perfect," Will said. He kissed her forehead.

Claire laughed, then gave him a kiss on the chin. "How could it be more perfect?"

His gaze met hers. "You could marry me," Will suggested.

How was it that he always knew exactly what she was thinking, sometimes even before she did? Claire had been waiting for him to ask again. Every now and then, he'd find a silly reason to propose and up until now, she'd held him off. And she'd been confident that, when the time was right, he'd try again. Just yesterday she'd walked past a jeweler on Michigan Avenue and wondered what ring she'd choose from those displayed in the window. But now that Will had asked her, the ring didn't seem important at all.

"Well?" he asked. "Are you going to give me an answer?"

"Yes," Claire said.

"Yes, you're going to give me an answer? Or yes *is* your answer?"

"Both," Claire said. "Yes, I will marry you, Will Donovan, and yes, that is my answer."

A wide smile broke across his face and he blinked in disbelief. "All right then," Will said. "You finally said yes. We're going to get married. It's a plan."

"Yes," Claire replied. "I think we're safe saying that now, we definitely have a plan."

Will grabbed her by the waist and picked her up off the ground, hugging her until she let out a tiny scream. Claire braced her hands on his shoulders and looked down into his eyes, so full of love and desire. "Now I have a surprise for you," she said.

"What would that be?"

"Reach into the back pocket of my jeans."

Will set her back on her feet and did as he was told, withdrawing two tickets. "Chicago Cubs?"

"Baseball," she said. "I figured it was about time you became familiar with the game. It's opening day today. The first game of the season. It's a very big thing here in Chicago. A ritual. Kind of like Sorcha's Samhain celebration."

He examined the tickets closely. "Sweetheart, I know the game quite well. I've been hitting home runs since the first time we jumped into bed together."

"That's a whole different game," Claire said, tapping him on the nose with the tickets. "If you're going to marry a girl from Chicago, then you need to choose sides. You're either a Cubs fan or a Sox fan. You either like pan pizza or thin crust. You eat your hot dogs with mustard or ketchup. If you plan to make me happy for the rest of my life, then you need to know these things."

"What about the Bulls?"

"That's basketball," Claire explained. "Completely different sport from baseball."

"I was just thinking, since I'd mastered baseball, I might want to try a new game?" He glanced around. "Any game that requires dribbling, putting it in the hole and shooting sounds like something I could get into."

"You never stop thinking about sex, do you?" Claire asked.

"Of course I do," Will replied. "For at least a few

minutes every day I make an effort to think about work." He glanced around. "Speaking of sex, we own the place now. What do you think about christening it properly?"

Claire reached for the buttons of her blouse and slowly began to undo them. "All right. But if you want me to explain basketball, then I'm going to have to start with the layup," she said.

Will growled playfully as he helped her with the buttons. "Oh, sweetheart, I do love American sports."

* * * * *

Welcome to cowboy country...

Turn the page for a sneak preview of
TEXAS BABY
by
Kathleen O'Brien
An exciting new title from Harlequin Superromance
for everyone who loves stories about the West.

Harlequin Superromance—
Where life and love weave together in
emotional and unforgettable ways.

CHAPTER ONE

CHASE TRANSFERRED his gaze to the road and identified a foreign spot on the horizon. A car. Almost half a mile away, where the straight, tree-lined drive met the public road. He could tell it was coming too fast, but judging the speed of a vehicle moving straight toward you was tricky.

It wasn't until it was about two hundred yards away that he realized the driver must be drunk…or crazy. Or both.

The guy was going maybe sixty. On a private drive, out here in ranch country, where kids or horses or tractors or stupid chickens might come darting out any minute, that was criminal. Chase straightened from his comfortable slouch and waved his hands.

"Slow down, you fool," he called out. He took the porch steps quickly and began walking fast down the driveway.

The car veered oddly, from one lane to another, then up onto the slight rise of the thick green spring grass. It just barely missed the fence.

"Slow down, damn it!"

He couldn't see the driver, and he didn't recognize this automobile. It was small and old, and couldn't have cost much even when it was new. It was probably white, but now it needed either a wash or a new paint job or both.

"Damn it, what's wrong with you?"

At the last minute, he had to jump away, because the idiot behind the wheel clearly wasn't going to turn to avoid a collision. He couldn't believe it. The car kept coming, finally slowing a little, but it was too late.

Still going about thirty miles an hour, it slammed into the large, white-brick pillar that marked the front boundaries of the house. The pillar wasn't going to give an inch, so the car had to. The front end folded up like a paper fan.

It seemed to take forever for the car to settle, as if the trauma happened in slow motion, reverberating from the front to the back of the car in ripples of destruction. The front windshield suddenly seemed to ice over with lethal bits of glassy frost. Then the side windows exploded.

The front driver's door wrenched open, as if the car wanted to expel its contents. Metal buckled hideously. Small pieces, like hubcaps and mirrors, skipped and ricocheted insanely across the oyster-shell driveway.

Finally, everything was still. Into the silence, a plume of steam shot up like a geyser, smelling of rust and heat. Its snakelike hiss almost smothered the low, agonized moan of the driver.

Chase's anger had disappeared. He didn't feel anything but a dull sense of disbelief. Things like this didn't happen in real life. Not in his life. Maybe the sun had actually put him to sleep....

But he was already kneeling beside the car. The driver was a woman. The frosty glass-ice of the windshield was dotted with small flecks of blood. She must have hit it with her head, because just below her hairline a red liquid was seeping out. He touched it. He tried to wipe it away before it reached her eyebrow, though, of course that made no sense at all. Her eyes were shut.

Was she conscious? Did he dare move her? Her dress was covered in glass, and the metal of the car was sticking out lethally in all the wrong places.

Then he remembered, with an intense relief, that every good medical man in the county was here, just behind the house, drinking his champagne. He found his phone and paged Trent.

The woman moaned again.

Alive, then. Thank God for that.

He saw Trent coming toward him, starting out at a lope, but quickly switching to a full run.

"Get Dr. Marchant," Chase called. "Don't bother with 911."

Trent didn't take long to assess the situation. A fraction of a second, and he began pulling out his cell phone and running toward the house.

The yelling seemed to have roused the woman. She opened her eyes. They were blue and clouded with pain and confusion.

"Chase," she said.

His breath stalled. His head pulled back. "What?"

Her only answer was another moan, and he wondered if he had imagined the word. He reached around her and put his arm behind her shoulders. She was tiny. Probably petite by nature, but surely way too thin. He could feel her shoulder blades pushing against her skin, as fragile as the wishbone in a turkey.

She seemed to have passed out, so he put his other arm under her knees and lifted her out. He tried to avoid the jagged metal, but her skirt caught on a piece and the tearing sound seemed to wake her again.

"No," she said. "Please."

"I'm just trying to help," he said. "It's going to be all right."

She seemed profoundly distressed. She wriggled in his arms, and she was so weak, like a broken bird. It made him feel too big and brutish. And intrusive. As if touching her this way, his bare hands against the warm skin behind her knees, were somehow a transgression.

He wished he could be more delicate. But he smelled gasoline, and he knew it wasn't safe to leave her here.

Finally he heard the sound of voices, as guests began to run around the side of the house, alerted by Trent. Dr. Marchant was at the front, racing toward them as if he were forty instead of seventy. Susannah was right behind him, her green dress floating around her trim legs.

"Please," the woman in his arms murmured again. She looked at him, the expression in her blue eyes lost and bewildered. He wondered if she might be on drugs. Hitting her head on the windshield might account for this unfocused, glazed look, but it couldn't explain the crazy driving.

"Please, put me down. Susannah… The wedding…"

Chase's arms tightened instinctively, and he froze in

his tracks. She whimpered, and he realized he might be hurting her. "Say that again?"

"The wedding. I have to stop it."

* * * * *

Be sure to look for TEXAS BABY,
available September 11, 2007,
as well as other fantastic Superromance titles
available in September.

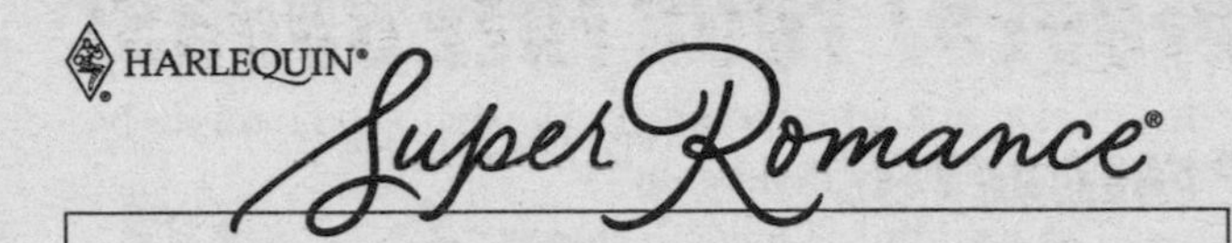
HARLEQUIN®
Super Romance®

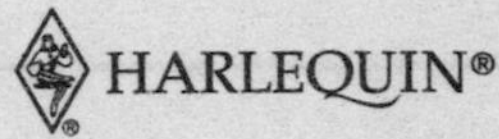

COMING NEXT MONTH

#345 KIDNAPPED! Jo Leigh
Forbidden Fantasies

She had a secret desire to be kidnapped and held against her will.... But when heiress Tate Baxter's fantasy game turns out to be all too real, can sexy bodyguard Michael Caulfield put aside his feelings and rescue her in time?

#346 MY SECRET LIFE Lori Wilde
The Martini Dares, Bk. 1

Kate Winfield's secrets were safe until hottie Liam James came along. Now the sexy bachelor with the broad chest and winning smile is insisting he wants to uncover the delectable Katie—from head to toe.

#347 OVEREXPOSED Leslie Kelly
The Bad Girls Club, Bk. 3

Isabella Natale works in the family bakery by day, but at night her velvet mask and G-string drive men wild. Her double life is a secret, even from Nick Santori, the club's hot new bodyguard who's always treated her like a kid. Now she's planning to show the man of her dreams that while it's okay to look, it's *much* better to touch....

#348 SWEPT AWAY Dawn Atkins
Sex on the Beach

Her plan was simple. Candy Calder would use her vacation to show her boss Matt Rockwell she was serious about her job. But her plan backfired when he invited her to enjoy the sinful side of Malibu. With an offer this tempting, what girl could refuse?

#349 SHIVER AND SPICE Kelley St. John
The Sexth Sense, Bk. 3

She's not alive. She's not dead. She's something in between. And medium Dax Vicknair wants her desperately! Dax fell madly in love with teacher Celeste Beauchamp when he helped one of her students cross over. He thought he was destined to live without her. But now Celeste is back—and Dax intends to make the most of their borrowed time....

#350 THE NAKED TRUTH Shannon Hollis
Million Dollar Secrets, Bk. 3

Risk taker Eve Best is on the verge of having everything she's ever wanted. But what she really wants is the handsome buttoned-down executive Mitchell Hayes, who must convince the gorgeous talk-show host to say "yes" to his business offer *and* his very private proposition....